I've travelled the world twice over,
Met the famous: saints and sinners,
Poets and artists, kings and queens,
Old stars and hopeful beginners,
I've been where no-one's been before,
Learned secrets from writers and cooks
All with one library ticket
To the wonderful world of books.

DUAL ENIGMA

Rosa Epton, solicitor, on her way home from Lewes Prison by train reads of a schoolboy, Jason Cutler, killed by a hit-and-run driver late at night and also witnesses a young girl sitting opposite her behaving erratically. A few days later the girl is reported missing, so although puzzled but not directly involved, Rosa carries on with her normal work. Until a client she has recently defended on a drugs charge is found murdered in the grounds of Jason's school. Could there be a connection?

Books by Michael Underwood
in the Ulverscroft Large Print Series:

CROOKED WOOD
MURDER WITH MALICE
A CLEAR CASE OF SUICIDE
DOUBLE JEOPARDY
HAND OF FATE
A PARTY TO MURDER
THE HIDDEN MAN
DEATH AT DEEPWOOD GRANGE
THE UNINVITED CORPSE
THE INJUDICIOUS JUDGE
DUAL ENIGMA

MICHAEL UNDERWOOD

DUAL ENIGMA

Complete and Unabridged

ULVERSCROFT
Leicester

First published in Great Britain in 1988 by
Macmillan London Ltd.

First Large Print Edition
published August 1990
by arrangement with
Macmillan London Ltd.
and
St. Martin's Press, Inc.,
New York

British Library CIP Data

Underwood, Michael, *1916–*
Dual enigma.—Large print ed.—
Ulverscroft large print series: mystery
Rn: John Michael Evelyn I. Title
823'.914[F]

ISBN 0-7089-2263-5

Published by
F. A. Thorpe (Publishing) Ltd.
Anstey, Leicestershire
Set by Rowland Phototypesetting Ltd.
Bury St. Edmunds, Suffolk
Printed and bound in Great Britain by
T. J. Press (Padstow) Ltd., Padstow, Cornwall

1

ALMOST everyone has a favourite season. For many it will be summer: for a few eccentrics, winter. But for the true connoisseurs of fickle British weather it will surely be spring or autumn.

Rosa Upton had never been in any doubt that autumn was her favourite time of year. She loved the smells and colours of that season, as well as the days of soft luminous light which put her in mind of the sleepy face of a waking child.

It was on such a day in October that she had travelled to Lewes to visit a client on remand in the prison there. It was a glorious day to be in the Sussex country-side, though Lewes prison would not in other circumstances have been her first choice of destination.

Her client (a born and bred Londoner who was seldom out of trouble, or, for that matter, out of prison) was apologetic about bringing her down from town. His previous offences had all been committed within the capital's generous bounds.

Her visit to the prison over, she found she had forty minutes before catching a train back to London. She wandered through the ancient town, stopping at a café for a cup of tea, after which she made her way to the station where she bought a local paper and sat on a seat at the end of the platform to read it. The late afternoon sun provided a welcome to an otherwise functional scene.

Her attention was caught by a piece on an inner page which she read with gathering interest. It seemed that the police were still seeking the driver of a car involved in a hit-and-run accident some three weeks before. The accident had taken place at the village of Oakway some ten miles west of Lewes and a schoolboy aged 12 with the name of Jason Cutler had been killed outright. Not only had the driver never been traced, but there was the added mystery of the boy's presence at the scene. The accident had occurred around nine or ten o'clock in the evening when, by rights, the boy should have been asleep in his dormitory. Instead he was at a lonely cross-road just beyond the perimeter of the school grounds, dressed in jeans and a wind-cheater over the top of his pyjamas. As yet no explanation had been forthcoming as to what he was doing when he met his death.

Rosa felt a sudden pang of sadness. She hadn't been particularly happy at boarding school herself and would have run away if it hadn't seemed such an impossible feat. Is that what Jason Cutler had been intent on doing?

Apparently not, for in the next paragraph she read that the headmaster, Mr. Richard Brigstock, described Jason as a happy, well-integrated twelve-year-old with no apparent problems. Moreover, he had been at Easter House School for two years, which posed the question, if he was unhappy, why had he left it so late to run away? And as though to acquit the school of any blame for what happened, the item mentioned that Jason was in charge of the boys' garden and was something of a green-fingered wizard.

Rosa finished reading the piece and sat wondering about the boy's death. Bad enough to die so young, but doubly terrible with a great question mark left hanging over the tragedy. There was mention of Jason's parents living in Egypt where his father worked for a multi-national firm of construction engineers. What a terrible shock it must have been for them when they received the news of their son's death.

Rosa was still brooding over this aspect of personal tragedy when her train was signalled. It was more crowded than she had anticipated and she made her way to a non-smoking compartment at the rear where she found a window seat vacant, apart from a crumpled newspaper lying on it. She glanced questioningly at the girl opposite. It might be her paper which she had discarded: on the other hand it might be a form of token occupation by somebody who had gone off to the buffet car.

"Excuse me, is this seat taken?" she enquired.

The girl, who was enveloped in a shapeless red sweater, made no reply and Rosa observed she was wearing a Walkman whose thin leads disappeared into a bulging carrier bag at her side. Rosa tapped her on the knee and pointed at the seat. The girl gave her an abstracted smile and leaned forward to remove the paper which she stuffed down the side of her seat. As Rosa settled herself, the girl dug into her carrier bag and produced a shiny apple which she proceeded to eat, core and all, until all she was left with was the stalk. After twiddling this between her forefinger and thumb in a ruminative sort of way, she dropped it into her bag.

Rosa reached into her briefcase and fetched out the paperback she had been reading. But then she laid it unopened on her lap and gazed out of the window at the changing pattern of green fields and clumplike woods, which would all too soon give way to the outer suburbs of London. From time to time she glanced across at the girl sitting opposite her, wondering what she was listening to on her headset. Her original assumption had been that it was music, but as the journey progressed she decided that music was unlikely to be responsible for so many variations of expression on the girl's face. Though her eyes were closed, she was clearly not asleep. So if it wasn't music, it must be words. A book, maybe, or a long, newsy tape from a friend who lived abroad. The latter would best explain her changes of expression, though enjoyment seemed to be behind them all.

As Rosa observed her, she became increasingly intrigued. It became a sort of game between them, albeit one of which the girl was blithely unaware. Unfortunately, it was also a game which Rosa had no chance of winning. She would never know how close her guesswork came to the truth.

On two occasions the girl opened her eyes and fumbled in the carrier bag, apparently turning the tape. After which she sat back again with a contented air.

Rosa reckoned she was in her early twenties at the most. She wore no make-up and had a generally fresh, healthy look about her. Her blonde hair was a mess, but somehow that seemed to go with the rest of her. She was naturally attractive without apparently bothering about her appearance and Rosa secretly envied her obvious confidence. She wondered where she came from and where she was bound for. She could easily be a girl sharing a flat with others in one of London's less fashionable enclaves. Equally, she might be a country girl living at home in rural Sussex; though there weren't too many of them around these days.

The journey was nearing an end and speculating about the girl's background had passed the time in a harmless way. Rosa put her unread book back in her briefcase and buttoned her jacket. The train was crossing the river on its approach to Victoria Station when, with startling suddenness, the girl tore off her Walkman and thrust it into the carrier bag. She had turned quite white and her expression had become one of undisguised alarm. Even as Rosa debated whether to say something to her, the girl leapt up from her seat and hastened along the aisle toward the door at the end of the compartment.

The last Rosa saw of her was jumping off the train as soon as it came to a halt and hurrying along the platform as if every second counted. By the time Rosa got out, the girl had vanished. She felt frustrated and strangely bereft. It was as though a seemingly happy story had been given a sudden shocking twist at the end.

As she queued for a taxi outside the

station, she found her mind totally preoccupied by what had just happened. She glanced about her in the forlorn hope that the girl might suddenly materialise. But she had vanished without leaving a single clue as to her identity.

The whole disturbing incident continued to haunt Rosa's thoughts during the rest of the day and when she reached home that evening. As a result, she found it hard to concentrate on the case she had to prepare for court the next day.

2

"AND how's Rosa this morning?"

Rosa turned to find Philip Atherly smiling at her. She had an urge to tell him that he had nothing to smile about. During a short acquaintance she'd had time to find out that he had more than his fair share of irritating habits and a supercilious smile was one of them. Another was the way he had addressed her by her first name, without either invitation or encouragement, almost from the first moment they had met, which had been at this very court. Rosa had been on the point of departure at the end of a case when he approached her.

"Care to defend me?" he had asked with the smile that now grated on her. "I heard you in court just now and knew at once you were the lawyer for me."

"What are you supposed to have done?" she had asked with a note of caution.

"Possession of a spot of cannabis. A lot

of nonsense about nothing if you ask me. Anyway, will you defend me?"

She should have been guided by her instinct and said no. But she was mildly flattered by his approach and, after all, as Robin Snaith, her senior partner, was fond of saying, lawyers are like cabs on a rank. They ply for hire.

That had been about a month ago, since when she had had a longish conference with him in her office and an exchange of telephone calls.

And now they had reached the day of his trial. He was due to plead guilty to a charge of possessing two grammes of cannabis and Rosa's task would be confined to mitigation of sentence.

"So how's everything?" he enquired again.

"All right," Rosa replied crisply. "And with you?"

"Fine. Also I've remembered to bring my chequebook." Observing Rosa's expression he added, "To pay the fine. I take it they'll accept a cheque?"

"Let's hope the court imposes a fine and nothing worse."

"You told me a fine was likely. Surely

10

people don't get sent to prison for having a bit of cannabis?"

"They can be. It depends on the circumstances. If the court took the view that you were a supplier, you'd almost certainly be put inside."

"But I'm not a supplier," he expostulated. "What I had was for my own use. For heaven's sake, Rosa, don't start scaring me now."

Rosa felt momentarily guilty. She had been unnecessarily brutal to him. Whatever her private doubts on the subject, he had all along maintained that he wasn't a drug pusher; moreover, he had not been charged with more than possession. Nevertheless she suspected that he knew more about the drugs scene than he was prepared to admit.

When she had asked him for personal particulars for the purpose of her plea in mitigation, he had been at pains to gloss over certain areas of his past. What was apparent was that he had had a considerable number of jobs over the last five years and he was still only 26. He had been a schoolmaster, a personal assistant to a senior partner in a firm of stockbrokers, a car salesman for a group that specialised in Mercedes and, most recently, had been a so-called executive with a firm of property developers on the Costa del Sol.

When Rosa had questioned him about his sources of income, he had told her that he was the beneficiary of a small trust fund which was sufficient to meet his basic needs, though no more. He also admitted to some savings and Rosa found herself wondering if they were profits from drug deals.

"Try and look contrite in court, even if you don't feel it," she said, as she noticed him smiling at a girl on the further side of the court lobby. "If there's one thing courts don't appreciate, it's a defendant who looks pleased with himself."

"How's this?" he said, pulling a face of mock gravity.

"I'm serious."

"Don't worry, I won't let you down."

"It won't be me but yourself that you let down."

The girl at whom he had been smiling had come over to where they were standing.

"This is Charlotte," Atherly said. "She's here to hold my hand."

"I've also brought some cash," Charlotte said, producing a bundle of £20 notes from her pocket. "Just in case they won't accept a cheque," she added.

"Rosa says they will take a cheque, always provided I'm not sent to prison."

"Oh surely not," the girl exclaimed, giving Rosa an anxious look.

"I was merely trying to get him to take the matter seriously," Rosa said with a touch of exasperation. "You may be better at it than I am. Possession of even a relatively small amount of cannabis is not a joking matter. Not these days, anyway. Courts have got really tough on drug offenders."

"I've already promised I won't let you down," he said, as though trying to pacify a querulous child.

"I suggest we go into court and wait for the case to come on," Rosa said firmly.

Even the smallest doses of her client's company were a strain. His whole manner irritated her. She tried to make allowances for clients who were facing the ordeal of a court appearance, but it was hard going where Philip Atherly was concerned.

As they moved towards the court, Rosa stepped aside to study the day's case list and to see which magistrate was sitting.

It was Mr. Wilfrid Fleetwood, known to all the regulars as Uncle Wilf. He was a charming, silver-haired old man who treated everyone with extreme courtesy and who had miraculously avoided becoming corrupted by an insidiously corrupting job. To say that he was also a good magistrate would have been going too far. He hated sending anyone to prison and still believed he could find good in everyone.

To defendants, he was a gift from heaven: to the police, a running sore. They would gladly have foregone all his courtesy for a more abrasive approach, even if that meant an occasional flick of the lash across their own shoulders.

As Rosa took her seat, the magistrate gave her a courtly smile, then peered with a benign expression around his court, as though everyone present had come to help him get through the day.

It wasn't long before the case was called

on and Philip Atherly stepped into the dock. He pleaded guilty to the charge of possessing cannabis and a nervous young woman from the crown prosecution service rose to present the facts. Nervousness gave her voice a certain strident quality and she gesticulated so as to give the impression of an unco-ordinated marionnette. When she resumed her seat, Mr. Fleetwood thanked her for her help in what he described as this serious matter.

After a police officer had given evidence of the defendant's antecedents—or as much of them as Atherly had been prepared to disclose—the magistrate turned towards Rosa.

"And what would you like to say to me, Miss Epton?" he enquired, as though it were the moment for which he had been waiting all morning.

"The first thing to tell your worship is that my client has learnt his lesson. In pleading guilty to this charge he has made a commitment to have nothing further to do with drugs of any sort." Rosa was thankful that Atherly was sitting behind her and that she was unable to observe his expression as she made this ringing

15

assertion. Admittedly it was what he had told her, but with more calculation than conviction.

Rosa went on, "The next important thing to tell your worship is that my client had the drug purely for his own use. He is not a pusher, nor has he been involved in the profit-making side of drug abuse. He has, he tells me, smoked cannabis on perhaps half a dozen occasions when he has been out with friends, but this was the first time he has ever had a quantity of the drug actually in his own possession. He very foolishly bought it from a man he met at a party whom he had neither seen before nor has seen since. He had been depressed in his search for a new job and sought to forget his problems in this stupid way. He is glad now that the police raided the party when they did, as it has given him the opportunity of reflecting on his foolishness before he was drawn deeper into the evil morass of the drug scene of today.

"There are just two further points I should like to make to your worship. The first is that my client is a person of hitherto good character and the second that he is still a young man. Young enough to benefit from leniency and to make good in life if your worship will give him the opportunity."

"Thank you, Miss Epton. Most helpful," Uncle Wilf said, giving her another courtly smile.

Atherly was prodded to his feet by the jailer and the magistrate addressed him.

"I'm glad to hear that you now realise what a foolish young man you have been. Anyone who dabbles in drugs has to be, at the very least, foolish. You are fortunate, however, in having had Miss Epton to plead on your behalf.

"I accept that you had the cannabis purely for your own purpose and that you acquired it at a time of personal stress, though I would remind you, if reminder still be necessary, that the taking of drugs, even of so-called soft drugs, has never solved anyone's problems.

"However, as Miss Epton has pointed out, you're a young man of hitherto unblemished character and I like to think that you now see the error of your ways and will make a determined effort to stay out of future trouble. In those circumstances, I do not consider that a custodial sentence is called for and I impose a fine of £300, which will, I hope, bring home to you the seriousness of your offence."

Philip Atherly bowed his head in what might have been taken as a sign of contrition, but was more likely to hide his expression of relief. At the same time the court inspector and the jailer exchanged routine glances of resignation and despair.

"Coming in front of Uncle Wilf is like being given the free run of a supermarket," the jailer was fond of saying.

Philip Atherly and Charlotte were waiting outside the court when Rosa emerged.

"There! I behaved perfectly, didn't I, Rosa?" Atherly said with a supercilious grin. "I said I wouldn't let you down."

"It might be more to the point to say thank you," Charlotte remarked with a touch of asperity. "But for Rosa, you might have gone to prison."

"Not in front of that old sheep. They told me he never puts anyone inside if he can help it."

"Oh, you're hopeless," Charlotte said crossly. She held out a hand to Rosa. "I'd

18

better take him home. Let me say thank you on his behalf."

"I love it when she gets all school-mistressy," he said to Rosa with a further grin. "Anyway, thanks for what you did for me. Till we meet again . . ."

If Rosa could help it, there'd certainly be no meeting again.

3

FOR Rosa the week that followed was exceptionally busy. She was in court every day and when she got back to her office there were conferences with clients. The result was that she was obliged to spend three or four hours working at home each evening.

She was used to these hectic spells and didn't mind provided they were of limited duration.

Fortunately, it was a week in which she was free of social engagements, so that there wasn't the added pressure of having to work late into the night.

Peter Chen, with whom she still had an enjoyable relationship, was in Singapore on business and was not due back until the following week. She liked Peter very much and always missed him when he was away. For the time being their affair was on an emotionally even keel and she hoped it might remain that way.

He had phoned her several times from

the other side of the world. She liked hearing his voice and was uplifted by his ability to sound both casual and intense at one and the same time.

It was exactly one week after Philip Atherly's appearance in court that she went along to her partner's room late one afternoon for a chat. She had just spent an hour with a particularly difficult client and needed to relax. She knew that Robin was in and not engaged as he had called her half an hour earlier wanting to come along to her room for the same purpose.

She found him sitting at his desk with an evening paper open in front of him.

"What's happening in the world?" she asked, dropping down gratefully into his visitor's chair. "I've scarcely looked at a paper for two days."

"The news is always the same," he remarked with a smile, "it's only the back-cloth which changes." He paused. "I thought there might be something about a case I did this morning, but there isn't."

"Which case was that?"

"The case of Lady Harriet and her father's forged cheques."

"People with titles usually make the news when they're in trouble."

"Presumably earls' daughters are no longer as newsworthy as they were. Possibly one of tomorrow's dailies will carry a report." He gave Rosa a paternalistic glance. "When are you expecting Peter home?"

"At the beginning of next week."

"Ah!"

"Is that meant to be a significant 'ah'? Anyway, I thought you liked him."

"I do. He's a charming person."

"But you don't really approve of my associating with someone who is Chinese, is that it?"

Robin sighed. That was exactly it. For all his charm and western ways, Peter was a hundred per cent Chinese, having been born of wealthy parents in Hong Kong, but largely brought up in England. Robin had never denied his paternalistic feelings towards Rosa whom he had originally taken on as a clerk and whose career he had carefully nurtured ever since. From time to time her private life had caused him qualms for she seemed to have a perverse instinct to flout convention. At least, that was how he saw it. Fortunately, her various unsuitable boyfriends had come and gone, leaving her apparently unscarred. Peter Chen was admittedly in a different category from the run of somewhat amoral young men she'd had in tow at one time or another and Robin had absolutely nothing against him other than the colour of his skin when related to the possibility of his marrying Rosa.

"Look, Robin," Rosa now said. "If you're worried at the thought of me and Peter getting married and producing pale yellow babies, forget it. We're both quite happy with our lives as they are. It's not even as if we actually lived together. We're no more than weekend lovers."

"I'm sorry," Robin said in a slightly ashamed tone. "I didn't mean to sound critical. I really do like Peter very much. And so does Susan."

"And Peter likes you both, so now we can all live happily ever after," Rosa said with the trace of a smile.

She was extremely fond of her senior partner and was always ready to acknowledge how much she owed him both in her career and generally. But that didn't mean she would allow him or anyone else to dictate to her about her private life.

During the next twenty minutes she and Robin discussed a whole range of subjects, including salary rises for Stephanie, their indispensable receptionist cum telephonist, and Ben, their junior all purposes clerk. They finished with an exchange of views on two recent judicial appointments, agreeing that one was as good as the other was disastrous.

It was as Rosa got up to go back to her room that her eye alighted on the paper which lay open on Robin's desk. She gave a sudden startled cry.

"I know that face."

"Who? This girl who's been abducted?"

"It's the girl I sat opposite in the train last week. The one I told you about."

Robin frowned. "Are you sure?"

"Positive. Her face has been haunting me ever since. Did you say she'd been abducted?"

"Read it for yourself," he said, pushing the paper towards her.

For several seconds Rosa just stared at the photograph. The paper had presumably got hold of a snapshot, but the girl's features were unmistakable. The wind-blown hair, the country-fresh look and the eyes which gave her face an expression of private amusement.

The caption beneath the photograph read: "Katrina Forbes aged 18 who, her parents fear, may have been abducted."

Beneath that came a paragraph which Rosa now read.

Mr. and Mrs. Alec Forbes of Northampton fear that their daughter may have been abducted. Katrina, known to all her friends as Trina, was last seen eight days ago. She was due to spend the weekend at her parents' home, but never arrived. It now transpires that she hasn't been seen at the hostel in Purefoy Street, WC1, where she lodged since she went down to Sussex for the day last Wednesday. She did, however, phone the next day to say she wouldn't be back for a few days as she was going home for a long weekend. Mrs. Patricia Forbes, her mother, says, "Trina's a very sensible, level-headed girl and we can't understand why she hasn't been in touch with us. We are naturally worried and urge her to call us and let us know she's all right as soon as possible." Trina had been living in London for the past eight months where she'd had a variety of temporary jobs, the latest as a sales assistant at one of the Youth Today chain of shops. Inspector Gainham at Clerkenwell Police Station would like to hear from anyone who may have information as to Trina's whereabouts. He added that even though there was no firm evidence of physical harm having befallen her, the police couldn't rule out the possibility that she had been abducted and were anxious to trace her. Trina's father is a waterboard engineer and her mother, an attractive 38-year-old, works for a building society.

"It's definitely her," Rosa said numbly at the end. "What do you think I should do, Robin?"

"If you really are one hundred per cent certain, you should get in touch with the police. Her curious behaviour in the train followed within twenty-four hours by her disappearance would seem to be more than a coincidence."

Rosa shook her head in a mystified fashion. "What on earth was on that tape to have caused such an abrupt change in her manner?"

Robin nodded towards his telephone. "Ask Stephanie to put you through to Inspector Gainham."

"That's most interesting, Miss Epton," Inspector Gainham said when Rosa finished speaking. "You are quite sure, I suppose, that she was the girl sitting opposite you in the train?"

"Quite certain. As soon as I saw the photograph in the paper, I recognised her. Incidentally, have you found out what she was doing down in Sussex that day?"

"She told a girl at the hostel she was going to see a friend, but no more than that. So far our enquiries on that score have drawn a blank. But now we know she was on that particular train back to London, we may be able to discover where she boarded it. I may say her parents are unaware of her having any friends who live in Sussex. She usually went home to

Northampton every six weeks or so and was expected last weekend, but never turned up. When Mrs. Forbes phoned the hostel on Saturday she was told her daughter had called on Thursday morning to say she was going home for a long weekend. Whether that was a deliberate lie or she really was intending to go home, we simply don't know."

"It could mean the difference between her being a voluntary missing person and her having been forcibly abducted."

"Quite so. Her parents are insistent that she wouldn't just go off without a word to anyone."

"Parents don't always know what their eighteen-year-old daughters get up to in London."

"I agree. Even so there's something strange about the manner of her disappearance. Even stranger in the light of what you've just told me."

"What about the shop where she worked, can't anyone there help?"

"It was her first week of work at that particular shop and Wednesday was her day off. They're open seven days a week. They were a bit cross when she didn't turn up on Thursday morning, but they're not unused to that sort of thing from their casual staff." He paused and went on, "Did you notice, Miss Epton, whether she beat any sort of time with her hands or feet while she was listening to the tape?"

"You mean, as if she were listening to music?"

"Yes."

"No, she didn't."

"It's not conclusive of course, but . . ."

"I can't think that music would have caused such changes of expression of her face."

"It could have been someone singing. Amusing lyrics, something of that sort."

"That possibility hadn't occurred to me," Rosa remarked thoughtfully. "I still believe it's more likely she was listening to a tape made by a friend."

"So what did the friend say to make her tear off the headset in apparent alarm?"

Rosa sighed. "I wish I knew. Heaven knows I've thought about it enough. It was obviously something dramatic and start-ling. I suppose it might have been a threat of some sort. As a result of which she's disappeared."

"A threat to herself, do you mean?"

"I've no idea. One can only speculate."

"And not very profitably, either," Inspector Gainham remarked with a sigh of his own. "I'm grateful for your information, Miss Epton, even if it deepens rather than clarifies the mystery of Trina's disappearance. Let's hope she turns up safe and sound—and soon."

Robin, who had been listening to the conversation on an extension, leaned back in his chair.

"I wonder what Trina Forbes was mixed up in?" he said in a ruminative tone. "Quite obviously something."

4

TOBY CUTLER had been devastated by his younger brother's death. Despite an eight-year age difference, they had always been bound by a strong bond of affection.

When their parents moved to Egypt where Mr. Cutler was on a three year contract, it was agreed that Toby should attend a residential business studies college which was situated within comfortable distance of Easter House School where Jason had already been a pupil for a year. They reckoned he would like to feel his older brother was close by even if his parents were abroad. It was an arrangement that had several advantages, in particular the ease with which Toby could take Jason out from school on visiting days.

The circumstances of his brother's death had not only shocked Toby deeply at the time, but had continued to haunt him in the ensuing weeks.

As a matter of routine, the police had interviewed him to see if he could shed any light on his brother's unexplained presence at the scene of his death. But he had not been able to help them.

Mr. Brigstock, the headmaster of Easter House School, and Toby had always been on polite terms with one another, but had never established any rapport. The fact was that Mr. Brigstock was always on the defensive with adolescents and Toby fell near enough within that category.

The villagers of Oakway—at least, those who had any dealings with the school—reckoned his attitude was the result of having a flighty wife some twenty years younger than himself. It was said he was endlessly suspicious that people were making jokes about him behind his back.

The first Mrs. Brigstock had died three years previously and within twelve months he had married Sally Nairn, the twenty-one-year-old under-matron. Everybody had been taken by surprise, none more so than the chief matron who had promptly resigned.

At all events, Toby was considerably surprised when he received a phone call from Mr. Brigstock one evening asking him if he would come to the school the next day.

"I suggest about six o'clock," the headmaster said. "The boys will be doing their prep and it's one of the quieter periods of our school day. I shall be pleased to offer you a glass of sherry."

Toby felt he had no choice but to accept the invitation. It was obviously something to do with Jason's death, but what? Exactly four weeks had gone by since that tragic event. The funeral was over and his parents had returned to Egypt after a flying visit to England. Meanwhile, the police were no further forward in their efforts to trace the driver.

Boys of twelve don't leave wills and complicated estates to be settled, so what did Mr. Brigstock want? Jason's few personal possessions had already been disposed of and Toby had kept for himself the small gold St. Christopher medal that had failed so wretchedly to protect his brother from danger.

Toby timed his arrival the next evening for ten minutes past six. By the time he parked his car he was feeling faintly resentful and truculent and wished he was somewhere else. And yet he knew it wasn't an invitation he could have refused.

To his surprise the front door was opened by Sally Brigstock.

"Hello, Toby," she said with a pleased smile. "Is Richard expecting you?"

"Yes. He phoned me yesterday and asked me to come over."

"He's probably in his study. What's he want to see you about, or shouldn't I ask?"

"I've no idea. He didn't say."

"I'm sure there was the offer of a glass of sherry?" she said with a giggle.

"Yes, that was mentioned."

"I'm afraid you won't get the Spanish; that's only for very important parents. It'll be South African or Cyprus sherry for you."

"I don't like the stuff anyway."

"Nor do I. Though I have to pretend to —as well as a lot of other things." Her expression became momentarily clouded. "I miss Jason terribly. He was a love of a boy. It's awful that the police have never found out who did it."

A door opened along the corridor to their left and Mr. Brigstock appeared.

"Ah, there you are, Cutler. I was beginning to think you had got lost."

"It's my fault, Richard," his wife called out, then added softly, "as usual." She gave Toby a conspiratorial wink before turning away.

Toby walked along the corridor to where the headmaster was waiting.

"A glass of sherry?" Mr. Brigstock said as soon as they were in his study.

"I'd prefer a beer if you have any."

"Beer? I think there's a can of the stuff somewhere at the back of the cupboard. Never been a beer drinker myself."

Toby noticed that he poured himself a glass of Tio Pepe from a bottle that was also at the back of the cupboard. Presumably the bottles were shuffled around according to the status of the visitor he was expecting.

Toby accepted his glass of beer and waited for the headmaster to speak. He felt under no obligation to take the initiative. Let Mr. Brigstock declare his business.

"I was speaking to the police again yesterday," the headmaster said, after portentously clearing his throat. "They don't seem any nearer discovering the identity of the person who was driving the car. I just don't understand it. Presumably the car had to undergo repairs, so why hasn't any garage come forward and reported the matter?"

"There could be several answers to that," Toby said. "There are always back-street repairers who'll undertake work and not ask any questions, if the money's right."

"If that's true, it's a disgraceful state of affairs. But there must also be others who are holding back information."

"Who do you mean?"

"Associates and acquaintances of the driver."

Toby shrugged. "Possibly."

After a pause, Mr. Brigstock went on in a stiff voice, "There are all manner of unpleasant rumours going around the village. That's what I really wanted to speak to you about. Maybe you've heard them?" Toby shook his head and the head-master continued, "I believe you frequent the Pheasant public house in Oakway from time to time?"

"I've been in there, but I certainly don't frequent it."

"Oh! Anyway, you know the place?"

"Yes, but I haven't picked up any rumours when I've been there."

"It's being said that your brother was running away from school because he was unhappy. That he was being bullied and was homesick." He fixed Toby with a firm look. "You and I both know that's rubbish." When Toby didn't immediately reply, he went on fiercely, "It's quite untrue and I'd like you to help quash all such defamatory talk. It damages the school's reputation and that's something I won't tolerate." He paused and his tone was quieter when he continued. "Did your brother ever complain to you about being bullied or being unhappy here?"

"No, never."

"When you saw him, did he always seem perfectly settled and content?"

"Yes."

"I know you had a close relationship with him, so that if he had been unhappy, he'd have let you know soon enough, wouldn't he?"

"I think so," Toby said a trifle warily.

"Did he ever mention the possibility of running away?"

"No."

Mr. Brigstock gave a theatrical sigh. "Well, that's what they're saying in the village and it's a monstrous calumny. No boy has ever run away from Easter House. Moreover, if that had been his intention, is it likely he'd have gone off in his pyjamas with only a pair of jeans and a jacket pulled over them?" He paused and slowly raised his eyes until they met Toby's. "It's my belief he sneaked out of the dormitory to meet someone."

Toby looked startled. "Meet who?"

"I hoped you might be able to answer that question. After all, you knew him better than anyone."

Was Mr. Brigstock insinuating that he, Toby, had been involved in some way in his brother's death? It wasn't just his words, but the penetrating stare that accompanied them. Counter-attack, he had always been taught, was the most effective form of defence and there was no doubt in his mind that he was being called on to defend himself.

"Is that why you asked me over, in order to accuse me of knowing more about Jason's death than I've told the police?"

"My dear fellow," Mr. Brigstock broke in hastily, "please don't think I'm accusing you of anything. I was merely seeking to ascertain whether you might have some idea what your brother was doing out of bounds that evening?" Toby shook his head. "But you agree with my theory that he'd gone to meet somebody?" the headmaster said in a pressing tone.

"I suppose it's possible," Toby said doubtfully, "but only in the sense that anything's possible."

"There was that letter we found in his locker which had come a few days before his death. No address, but postmarked west London and simply signed P. You recall it?" Toby nodded and Mr. Brigstock continued, "It simply said: 'Dear Jason, Here's a fiver, keep up the good work. P.' What good work?" Mr. Brigstock asked bleakly. "And why didn't your brother hand in the money to me to be credited to his account? He knew that was the proper procedure." He paused and fixed Toby with another hard stare. "I'm sure you must have given the matter as much thought as I have, Cutler . . ."

"Certainly I have, but I still can't help.

Although Jason and I were close, that didn't mean he always told me everything. As to why he didn't hand in the £5, it's obvious he didn't wish to be questioned about it. Anyway, you found it in his locker, so he hadn't spent it."

Mr. Brigstock pursed his lips. "It was a regrettable lapse on his part," he said severely. "Moreover, until explained, it leaves a nasty taste in one's mouth. One doesn't like to think ill of the dead, especially of a twelve-year-old schoolboy, but . . ."

He left the sentence unfinished and Toby decided he had had enough. The headmaster's pedagoguish manner, not to mention his insinuations and oblique accusations, had become something he could do without.

"I must be getting back to college," he said abruptly, springing from his chair.

"Yes, of course. It was good of you to come. I hoped that, putting our heads together, we might have come up with some answers." The headmaster walked over to the door and paused with his hand on the handle. "I'm sure I can rely on you to quash any of the unpleasant rumours that are going around. About your brother running away because he was unhappy, I mean. If that had been the case, you'd have been the first to know."

Toby decided to ignore this veiled insinuation. "I can find my own way out," he said firmly, as Mr. Brigstock opened the door.

He had just reached the front door when he heard hurrying footsteps.

"Just off, are you?" Sally Brigstock said. She came to a halt in front of him and peered closely into his face so that he could smell her perfume. In other circumstances he might have made a pass at her, for she was deliberately flaunting her femininity at him.

"How did you get on with Richard?" she asked softly. "What did he want to talk to you about?"

Toby felt suddenly embarrassed by her proximity and the urgency of her manner. He didn't want her husband to emerge suddenly from his study and find them in whispered conversation at the front door.

"He just wondered if I had any fresh theories about Jason's death," he said, stepping back a pace.

"He's worried about a lot of silly rumours going around. Did he tell you that, too?"

"Yes."

"Jason wouldn't have been the first boy to run away from school," she said with a touch of petulance. "It's to be expected. After all, boarding schools are rather like prison and prisoners are always trying to escape."

Toby nodded, hoping to cut short any further conversation.

"And, anyway," she went on, "who cares what they're saying in the village? They've got to have something to gossip about. Poor little Jason! But wasn't he lucky to have such a nice big brother!" She gave Toby a quick kiss on the cheek and stook back observing his nonplussed expression with wry amusement.

As he walked back to his car, he tried to assemble his thoughts. It had been a strange visit. He had gone not knowing what to expect and was leaving with his mind in turmoil.

He reached the end of the half-mile drive and, on the spur of the moment, turned left for Oakway rather than right which was the direction of his college. He would visit the Pheasant and see if there was anything to be found out there.

The landlord of the Pheasant was one Jim Thesiger. He and his wife, Gina, were Londoners from Bethnal Green who had deserted the capital some seven years previously to avoid the further hassle of a running family feud that had lasted for the best part of a decade. They had no children and settled surprisingly well in their very different environment.

When Toby entered, Jim was just coming up from the cellar with a fresh keg of beer and Gina was talking to a customer at the farther end of the bar.

Though not a picturesque village pub, in the sense that there were no oak beams or horse brasses or open fires, it had its regular clientèle and Jim and his wife went out of their way to be welcoming. The fact that they were now totally accepted by the locals was the measure of their success.

"Evening," Jim said, putting the keg in position and glancing up at Toby on the other side of the counter. Then he frowned. "Don't I know your face? Been in 'ere before, 'aven't you?"

"Once or twice."

"I know you're not a regular, but I was sure I'd seen your face before. What are you drinking?"

"Half a pint of bitter."

"Got your car outside, 'ave you?"

"Yes."

"Thought so. Otherwise you'd be a pint man. Right?"

Toby smiled and nodded. "My name's Toby Cutler."

Jim Thesiger let out an exclamation.

"Got it! You're related to that poor little bugger who was run down and killed about a month ago?"

"He was my brother."

"Didn't reckon 'e could 'ave been your son, unless you'd started very young. Somebody's 'iding the bloke that killed 'im, that's for sure. I don't mean 'iding 'im in a cupboard or anything like that, but 'olding back on information." Toby leaned forward with a show of interest. "Mind you, I'm not surprised at the poor little bugger wanting to run away from that place. The 'eadmaster's got as much blood in his veins as a stick-insect. And as for that wife of his, I used to pick 'er sort up in Piccadilly on a Saturday night."

"The headmaster's quite sure my brother wasn't running away," Toby remarked.

"Then what was 'e up to? Answer me that." Toby shook his head helplessly. "Well, I 'ope they catch the bloke that did it. I know what I'd do to 'im. I'd make sure 'e'd never drive again."

"Take away his licence for life, you mean?"

The landlord gave a derisive snort. "I'd do something a darn sight more effective than that. People who kill kids with their cars, and don't even stop, deserve a taste of their own medicine."

Toby looked startled. "You don't literally mean an eye for an eye?"

"Why not? I'd castrate all sex offenders and hang murderers."

"But this person wasn't either. It could even have been a girl."

"Never! It was a bloke all right. Could 'ave been somebody from the school." Observing Toby's surprised expression, he

45

went on, "You 'adn't thought of that, 'ad you?"

"No."

"I wouldn't trust any of that lot. Wouldn't let any kid of mine go there to be taught. All 'e'd probably learn would be 'ow to cheat or become a queer."

"You make it sound an awful place. My brother always seemed quite happy there."

"It's not natural shutting boys up like battery 'ens," the landlord said darkly. "Anyway, I don't encourage any of the masters to do their drinking 'ere. Not after what 'appened."

"What did happen?" Toby asked, full of curiosity.

"One of their young masters borrowed two 'undred quid off me and the next thing I knew 'e'd left. Never saw 'im or my money again. I don't mind telling you I'd break 'is neck if 'e ever did show 'is face."

"How long ago was that?"

"A few years back, but I 'aven't forgotten 'is face. Nor 'as Colonel Fox."

"Who's Colonel Fox?"

"Owns most of the farmland 'ereabouts. The same young fellow put 'is daughter in

46

the family way. She was only sixteen at the time. 'Ad an abortion and all."

"They say that every barrel has at least one bad apple," Toby said, and then wished he hadn't.

"Drink that down and 'ave the other 'alf on me," Jim Thesiger said with a sudden switch of mood. "Got far to go, 'ave you?" Toby shook his head. "Then a pint of beer's not going to land you in trouble." The landlord drew two half pints and handed one to Toby. Raising his glass, he said, "Let's 'ope the bloke who killed your brother gets his just desserts. That's a toast we can both drink to."

5

EARLY in the following week Rosa made another trip to Sussex to visit her client in Lewes prison. It was the day that Peter Chen had been due back from Singapore, but he had phoned on Sunday to say that he was going on to Sydney and wouldn't be home for a further five days. He told Rosa that he loved her and was missing her very much. She assured him that his feelings were reciprocated, which was true.

In the days since she had spoken to Inspector Gainham she had searched the papers for further news of Trina Forbes, but there had been none until that very morning.

The train was no more than half full and she had just opened the paper she had bought at the station when she came upon the item.

"Missing girl alive and well," she read.

Beneath this mini headline appeared the following:

Eighteen-year-old Trina Forbes who vanished nearly two weeks ago has been in touch with her parents. Her letter has, however, only served to add to their anxieties about what has happened to her. Though postmarked London, she gave no address and merely told her parents she was all right and they weren't to worry about her. Her mother fears it may have been written under duress and urges her daughter to phone and say where she is. "It's an enormous relief to know she's alive," Mrs. Forbes told our reporter, "but now our worries are of a different sort." A police spokesman declined to say whether her disappearance was still the subject of enquiries. It seems likely, however, that their investigation will be, at least, scaled down.

Rosa laid down the paper and stared pensively out of the window. It was not a twist to the story that she had expected. She had felt certain that Trina would sooner or later turn up dead, the only question being how long it would take for her body to be found.

It had been twelve days ago that she had first—and last—set eyes on Trina.

It was a relief to know she was still alive, though that fact now added a new dimension to the mystery.

On arrival at Lewes she took a taxi to the prison. When she told the driver her destination, he chuckled.

"I could almost be running a shuttle service today," he said. "You're my third fare wanting to go there. The first was one of the prison staff, then a solicitor from London and now you."

"I belong to the second category."

"You a solicitor?" the driver asked in a tone of surprise as he took a look at her in his rear-view mirror.

"Yes."

"Well, I never . . . I mean, you don't look like one."

"We come in all shapes and sizes these days," Rosa observed. Then to change the subject, she said quickly, "Do you live in the town?"

"Yes and no. I have a place to sleep here, if you get my meaning, but my parents live in a village called Oakway, about eight miles out. I'm divorced," he added, as if to explain his living arrangements.

"I've heard of Oakway," Rosa said. "The last time I was down here I was reading in the local paper about a schoolboy at Oakway who'd been killed by a hit-and-run driver. Has he ever been caught?"

"No. Nor has anyone said what the boy was up to when he was run down."

"I assumed he was running away, though I recall the headmaster refuting that suggestion. But then I suppose he would."

"If he was running away, why wasn't he properly clothed, instead of a couple of things pulled over his pyjamas? If you want my opinion, he'd slipped out of his dormitory to meet someone. That's why he was dressed as he was. He was expecting to be back in bed before long."

Rosa was thoughtful for a while. "But who was he meeting and for what purpose?" she asked in a puzzled tone.

"He had an older brother at a college only a few miles from Oakway. It could have been him."

"I imagine the police will have investigated that possibility."

"Yes. He denies it, of course."

"And what about his car, assuming he has one, did that show any signs of damage?"

"No."

"So it doesn't sound as if it was big brother's car that killed him." She paused and frowned at the back of the driver's head. "I agree the running away theory becomes less plausible when one remembers he'd already been at the school a couple of years. One presumes he would have got over any homesickness by then. I also recall the headmaster describing him as a level-headed, well-adjusted boy who was in charge of the boys' garden."

"That's right. Mind you, the headmaster's main concern has been to avoid any scandal. He set enough tongues wagging when he married a girl half his age within twelve months of his first wife dying. The rumours are that the school is mortgaged up to the hilt and that numbers are dropping. Also a number of the tradespeople have had difficulty getting their bills paid."

"I can't see any of that as relevant to Jason Cutler's death."

"It mayn't be relevant to a lawyer's mind, but it all goes to show that Easter House School isn't all it might appear to be."

"Weren't any of the boys in Jason's dormitory able to throw light on his escapade?" Rosa asked.

"I gather they sleep in cubicles and young Cutler's was at one end nearest the door. Nobody heard him leave." He was silent for a while, then said, "I reckon there's somebody up there who's afraid of the truth coming out."

"From all you've said, that could only be the headmaster."

"However you look at it, it's a puzzling business," the driver said as he drew up outside the prison entrance.

From what Rosa had earlier read and now heard, it certainly was. It seemed that her visits to Lewes were set to provide her with teasing enigmas.

In an office not far away Sergeant Stephen Richards sat poring over a pile of witness statements. He was young and recently

53

promoted and Jason Cutler's death was the first major case of which he had day to day charge.

His initial optimism had given way to dogged determination as the days went by without any trace of the driver and car that had done this wanton deed.

As an ordinary human being with all the normal feelings, he was outraged by the driver's conduct. As a police officer, he was resolved not to give up in his efforts to bring the offender to justice.

He had personally interviewed dozens of witnesses and taken scores of statements. He still believed that an answer to the mystery lay somewhere in the pile of paper on his desk. Not the identity of the driver maybe, but a clue as to what Jason Cutler had been doing out of his dormitory that evening.

He was aware of the two rival theories. Namely that Jason had either been running away or was keeping a secret rendezvous with some unknown person. He had found himself favouring first one then the other.

He tended to share the village view of the headmaster of Easter House School.

Anyone with a flirtatious wife twenty years younger than himself automatically aroused a policeman's suspicions and his first encounter with Sally Brigstock had left him in no doubt that she was indeed a flirt.

He turned his attention to the statements of Jason's immediate contemporaries, the boys in his form and in his dormitory who, if anyone could, must surely be able to throw light on what had happened. Some had talked more than others. Some had obviously enjoyed what they saw as a moment of fame: others had been nervous and monosyllabic. But somewhere in all the outpourings must be a clue, which he, as a trained police officer, should be able to recognise.

He picked up the statement of Nicholas Youngman who was described as Jason's closest friend at the school. He was a year younger than Jason.

Jason Cutler was my best friend [the statement ran]. We got on because neither of us liked cricket or football. Jason wasn't allowed to play games because of his leg. He was in charge of the boys' garden and occasionally I helped him though I don't really know anything about plants. We used to play a lot of games like Monopoly and draughts together. I used to help Jason with his maths prep. He wasn't any good at maths and it's my best subject. I had no idea Jason was going out of the dormitory that night. He didn't tell me. Although he was my best friend, we didn't share all our secrets. As far as I know Jason wasn't homesick. He was very fond of his older brother Toby. I quite liked Toby.

Sergeant Richards looked up and frowned as he recalled taking that part of the statement. Nicholas had mentioned Toby Cutler and it was in reply to a direct question that he had said he "quite liked him". There had been a note of reservation in his voice, with a subtle emphasis of the word "quite".

At the time Richards hadn't pursued the point, but now he wondered. On the other hand there could be any number of harmless reasons for Nicholas not liking the older Cutler brother. Maybe he was made to feel the odd one out when the three of them were together. From all Richards had been told, Jason and his brother had had an exclusive relationship, which probably left others out in the cold. It was natural that Nicholas should blame Toby for this; for coming between him and his friend.

There wasn't much more to the statement, save for Nicholas's repeated denial of knowing what Jason was up to on the night he met his death. He had struck Sergeant Richards as a truthful, straightforward lad, though somewhat lacking in imagination. He had been shocked by his friend's death, but had not apparently shed any tears or suffered any subsequent reaction.

From all accounts Jason had been generally liked. He had an equable temperament and his attitude to life could be summed up by the dictum "live and let live", which was probably, Richards reflected, as good a recipe as any for survival at a boarding school. His friend's mention of Jason not being allowed to play football and cricket referred, Richards knew, to the osteomyelitis from which he had once suffered in his right leg. It had left the shin bone brittle and meant that he couldn't safely play any game involving the possibility of violent physical contact. Fortunately gardening had apparently absorbed his interests, though, in Richards's view, it was a poor substitute for playing football.

He turned to the statement of Peter Geoffrey Winslow, "schoolmaster, aged 34".

"Jason Cutler had been in my form (Ia) for the past three terms. He was an average pupil and a pleasant enough boy. He never exhibited any signs of homesickness and I'm at a complete loss to know what he was doing out of bounds on the evening he met his death. It goes to show that still waters run deep. I can think of nothing to explain his conduct. It is all a complete mystery, which is an uncomfortable admission to have to make."

So much for Jason's form-master, Sergeant Richards reflected as he tucked the statement away.

He extracted the letter which had been found in Jason's locker. Somebody signing himself simply as "P." had sent Jason £5 and exhorted him to keep up the good work.

He had submitted the letter to the laboratory for scientific examination and had only recently received the report. It told him there were a number of smudged fingerprints on the envelope which might help if they could ever be identified. The only identifiable print on the letter itself was Jason's. The writing had been made with a green ballpoint pen, but without a control sample, nothing further could be said about it.

None of which was any help in deciding what "good work" Jason had been up to. It was a colloquialism and might, of course, have been an exhortation to work hard at school, with a fiver enclosed as a bribe to do so. As a matter of routine, Richards had checked Jason's marks for the weeks preceding his death, but there was nothing about them to merit either a reward or a bribe. And the fact that Toby had been unable to tell the police who "P" was added to the mystery.

Richards had ascertained that incoming letters at the school were not subject to censorship. Outgoing mail was scrutinised by the second master who was responsible for putting stamps on the letters. Only if he came across a letter addressed to a dubious recipient were any questions asked. For example, a boy who had written to a firm of bookmakers found himself short of a satisfactory explanation and the letter was ceremonially destroyed.

The fact that the writer of Jason's letter gave no address and hadn't chosen to sign it with a name led Sergeant Richards to the irresistible conclusion that he was guarding against it falling into wrong hands. But what, if anything, did that have to do with Jason's death? Richards wished he knew.

He reached for the pathologist's report. According to Dr. Evershed, Jason had been struck by a fast-moving vehicle while he was crossing the road and had sustained multiple injuries from which he had died immediately. Hardened though Sergeant Richards was, he felt sickened by the list of appalling injuries inflicted on Jason's body. The force of the impact had catapulted him forward some twenty yards, where he came to rest on the verge at the side of the narrow road. As the pathologist succinctly put it, "the body was severely mutilated".

Where had the driver come from and where was he bound for on this misty evening in early October? Where it happened was the intersection of two minor roads, which were used mainly by people who lived in the area. The various marks caused by the accident had been photographed and measured and studied by Richards until he knew them better than the contours of his own face. They did nothing, however, to help him solve the two most puzzling aspects of the case.

He suddenly turned his attention again to the enigmatic letter which had accompanied the £5. He had all along been assuming the "P" must be a male. But was even that a safe assumption?

6

SALLY BRIGSTOCK screamed and screamed, her screams becoming wild sobs as she fled across the field towards the distant lights of the school. Fled from the dead man whom she had discovered lying on the floor of the old summer-house, with a face that was no longer a face but a shapeless mass of red pulp.

As she reached the side door of the school it opened and Peter Winslow peered out. She flung herself against him, clutching him by the waist to prevent herself slithering to the ground.

"What on earth's happened?" he asked anxiously as he supported her.

"There's a dead man in the old summer-house," she gasped.

"A dead man? Who?" His tone was aggressively suspicious for he regarded the headmaster's wife as having the sort of imagination that saw dead bodies without necessarily being stretched to its limit.

"It was horrible, Peter," she said between sobs. "His head . . . he was . . . you couldn't recognise him."

Winslow frowned, still unsure what to believe.

"Better come in and sit down," he said. "I'll get you a drink. Your husband won't be back from his meeting yet."

He guided her along the school's deserted corridors. It was just after nine o'clock and the boys were all upstairs in their dormitories.

They reached the headmaster's study and entered. It would be at least another hour before Richard Brigstock returned from the regular monthly meeting of the local Natural History Society of which he was a keen member.

Peter Winslow went across to the cupboard in which he knew the drink to be kept and poured a neat brandy for Sally and a large Scotch for himself.

"Here, drink this," he said. He watched her take a cautious sip, followed by a larger one. "Tell me again exactly what you found in the old summer-house."

"You don't believe me, do you, Peter?

I've told you, there's a dead man lying on the floor."

"Who?" he asked, his tone still suspicious. It wasn't April Fool's Day and Hallowe'en was past. Even so . . .

"He didn't have a face any more, just an eye hanging out," she said and started to cry noisily again.

"Might it have been someone from here?"

"How do I know?" she shouted angrily. "For heaven's sake, do something."

Peter Winslow departed. The sooner he discovered for himself what had happened, the better. He raced upstairs to Matron's small sitting-room. Judy was new that term and was watching television when he knocked on her door and burst in. He told her briefly that Sally Brigstock had found someone badly hurt in the old summer-house and was having hysterics in her husband's study. Would she therefore go down and stay with her while he went off to investigate?

What Sally herself chose to tell Matron was up to her, though it occurred to him that, sooner rather than later, somebody was going to ask her what she was doing at the old summer-house on a dank November night.

Meanwhile, he dashed down to the kitchen area where Fred, the caretaker and general factotum, had his room. Fred was solid and sensible and Winslow just prayed that he'd also be sober at that hour of the evening. Fortunately he was and readily agreed to accompany him.

"Thought I heard a shot a while back," he remarked as they set out. "I was just coming up from the boiler room."

"It might have been a car backfiring," Winslow said in a half-hopeful tone.

Fred threw him a pitying glance. "Not all that uncommon to hear the occasional shot round here, even at night. Doesn't necessarily mean trouble."

"What time would it have been?"

"About an hour ago."

"That would make it around eight thirty."

"It wasn't long after Mr. Brigstock went out. Did Mrs. Brigstock have any idea who the dead man was?"

"She said his face had been blown away and he was unrecognisable."

"Could have been a poacher," Fred said

in a thoughtful voice, as they hurried across the last field before reaching the old summer-house. "I did hear at the Pheasant that Colonel Fox had set up some booby-traps on his land to keep off poachers."

"He'd hardly have booby-trapped the old summer-house which isn't on his property. Anyway, it's illegal to set up lethal contraptions to protect your land."

"It's his field just the other side of the lane," Fred said. "The chap could have been injured there and have staggered across. As to it being illegal, I don't think that would have worried the Colonel. He's a law unto himself when it comes to looking after his rights."

"Well, we'll soon know," Winslow said grimly, as they made out the outline of the summer-house ahead.

He was carrying a flashlight and had the beam trained on the uneven ground as they hurried towards their goal.

The old summer-house was close to a hedge which separated the field from the lane beyond and marked the school's boundary. It was a wooden structure enclosed on three sides and with a bench running round its inside walls. It had been dumped in a corner of the field by a previous owner of Easter House before it became a school and had remained there ever since. Unused, but inoffensive.

They reached the open side and Winslow shone the torch inside.

"Oh, my God!" he exclaimed, falling back a pace at the horrific sight which met his eyes.

"Here, give me the torch," Fred said in a calm, practical tone. He stared down at the figure lying on its back on the floor. "Looks like he got a barrel-load of shot in his face at close range," he went on, peering more closely, while Peter Winslow felt as if he was going to be sick.

"Thank God it's not anyone we know," he said weakly.

"I can recognise him all right," Fred said.

"Who is it, for heaven's sake?"

"A young chap who taught here for a couple of terms before you came. Name of Atherly."

7

AS had happened before, it was Ben, Snaith and Epton's alert young clerk who brought to notice a newspaper item affecting one of the firm's clients.

"Seen this, Miss E.?" he asked eagerly as he shot into Rosa's room soon after lunch the next afternoon. He laid a mid-day paper on her desk and pointed at a paragraph headed, "Man Shot". "It's that bloke you defended the other day on a drugs charge," he went on. "Can't be two Philip Atherlys walking around. Not that this one'll be doing any more walking after what's happened to him."

It wasn't a long piece, but it was sufficient to excite Rosa's interest. It was not so much the fact that Atherly had been murdered which aroused her curiosity (after all, he had been a one-off client whom she had hoped never to see again) as the place where it had happened. "In

68

the grounds of a school at Oakway in Sussex", the paper said.

Though the school wasn't named, Rosa hadn't the slightest doubt that it must be Easter House and if that were so, it became an extraordinary coincidence how often that establishment had recently impinged upon her mind.

"I agree, Ben," she said, looking up, "it must be the same person."

"You didn't much go for him, did you?"

"No. I found him fairly insufferable."

"It says the police are treating his death as murder and are hopeful of an early arrest. Means they obviously know who did it."

"Or think they know," Rosa said with a smile. "Anyway, I wonder who it was?"

"And why?"

"Yes, that too," she said with another smile. There was something infectious about Ben's zestful interest in all that was going on.

"Perhaps you'd like to keep the paper," he said as he prepared to go. "Meanwhile, anything you want me to do?"

"I can't think of anything, Ben. I don't

suppose we'll have to wait long before the papers tell us a bit more."

In the event, the wait was less than that. Not long after Ben had departed, Stephanie came on the line.

"There's a Charlotte Bailey would like to speak to you, shall I put her through?"

"Charlotte Bailey?" Rosa said, uncertainly. "Do I know her?"

"She says she met you at court when you defended Philip Atherly," Stephanie said in the dry, expressionless voice she used on the phone.

"Oh, that Charlotte! I don't think I ever knew her other name. Yes, Steph, put her through," Rosa said with a sharp tingle of interest.

"Miss Epton? I don't know if you remember me, but I came to court with Philip Atherly that day," Charlotte said as soon as the connection was made.

"Yes, of course I remember."

"You've heard what's happened to Philip?"

"Somebody showed me an item in a midday paper. That's all I know."

"Did it say he'd been murdered?"

"Yes."

There was a pause before Charlotte spoke again. "I think it would be best if I were to come and see you," she said at length.

"Of course," Rosa said in a sympathetic voice. "But you realise he ceased to be my client on conclusion of the case. I'm not exactly sure how I can help you . . ."

"It was his explicit wish that I should get in touch with you if anything happened to him," Charlotte said. "May I come this afternoon? I'll explain everything then."

Charlotte looked strained but in full control of her emotions as she sat in Rosa's visitor's chair an hour later.

"Do you mean he was expecting something to happen to him?" Rosa asked, picking up their conversation where it had ended.

"Yes, he had been for some while."

"That sounds extraordinary. Surely he wasn't expecting to be murdered?" Rosa said incredulously.

"He was expecting some sort of physical attack and thought it might end in his death."

"Attack by whom?"

71

Charlotte let out a heavy sigh. "I don't know all the details. What I'm about to tell you is a mixture of fact and supposition. About three years ago, Philip spent a couple of terms teaching at a boys' prep school—"

"Was that Easter House School at Oakway?"

"Yes. He got the push when the headmaster discovered that Philip was having an affair with his recently wed wife. I gather she was near enough Philip's age and much younger than her husband. Knowing Philip, I'd be surprised if she was the only female in his sights while he was there." She gave a small reflective smile as she went on, "He just happened to be born heavily over-sexed. Anyway, he's gone on seeing Sally, that's the headmaster's wife, since he left the school. It was nothing regular. Sometimes she'd come up to London and Philip would book a room for a few hours at one of those cheap hotels near the station. But more often he'd drive down there and they'd meet and . . . well, I'm not sure where they'd go. Probably behind a hayrick in summer and in the back of the car in winter. Philip wasn't fussy."

"And then the day came when her husband found out?"

Charlotte gave a resigned shrug. "Philip was never very subtle. He was a prototype extrovert most of the time I knew him."

"When was it he told you that he thought he was a potential victim of assault?"

"About six weeks ago."

Rosa looked thoughtful. "But he'd been carrying on with Sally Brigstock far longer than that."

"I know. I assume it was around then that her husband first got wind of what was happening."

"So how did I come to be mentioned?" Rosa asked after a pause.

"It was after the case. Despite his maddening attitude, he was very impressed by what you did for him. It was a few days later when we were having a drink in a pub, he said quite suddenly, 'Should I get pushed off my perch, get Rosa Epton to investigate.' When I asked him what he was talking about, he merely said he believed somebody was after him."

"Did he ever refer to the matter again?"

"I kept on trying to question him about it, but he was always evasive, except to repeat that he meant what he'd said."

"If he thought he was in personal danger by continuing his liaison with Sally Brigstock, why did he go on?" Rosa asked in a puzzled tone. "It would not only have seemed foolhardy, but turned out to be so."

"I know. I can only say it was in keeping with his generally heedless attitude towards life."

"How long had you known each other?"

"About a year."

"Were you planning to get married?"

"Good gracious no. All things considered, we got on pretty well, but marriage was never part of the scheme."

"You weren't jealous of the other women in his life?"

"There was no point. I just accepted the situation. It meant I wasn't tied down either. Anyway, I don't have a jealous nature."

Rosa stared deep in thought at her desk. At length she looked up and said, "I still don't know what I'm supposed to investigate."

"Philip's death."

"What is there to investigate? On the face of it, he was killed by a jealous husband who found out that his wife and Philip had resumed their affair and decided to seek revenge. The next day or two will show whether that's right. But assuming that the headmaster is charged with Philip's murder, what is there to investigate?" She paused. "And there's another aspect, my time is money. Who's going to foot my bill?"

"Philip entrusted me with £2000 specifically for that purpose. He sold his Mercedes a few weeks ago and bought a second-hand Ford Fiesta which left him with quite a bit of cash in hand."

Rosa stared at her in astonishment. That presupposed he not merely believed he might be a walking target for someone. He knew. And yet he still strolled into the lion's den.

What was Rosa expected to achieve? And, more immediately, where did she begin?

8

DETECTIVE CHIEF INSPECTOR YULE had been about to have (for him) an early night when he had been called out to the scene of the murder.

He was a painstaking officer with an infinite capacity for detail and he didn't approve of police officers maintaining a high public profile. As a result he had never become a darling of the press.

He liked to make sure that all Ts were crossed and Is dotted before he charged a suspect. Not for him the quick arrest followed by a search for evidence to support it. Nevertheless he was generally respected, if grudgingly so, by colleagues with a more flamboyant style.

It was shortly after ten thirty when he reached Oakway and was led to the old summer-house by one of the patrol car officers who had arrived first on the scene. It didn't take even Yule long to become satisfied that he had a case of murder on his hands. The absence of any weapon proved that and it was the first thing he had looked for. In the course of his career he had come across a number of suicides where the dead person had chosen to kill himself by placing the muzzle of a shotgun in his mouth and pulling the trigger. It had always struck him as a singularly messy and inconsiderate way of going about things.

"There's a car parked up a track about a hundred yards along the lane, sir," one of the officers at the scene said. "Could be the deceased's."

Yule bent down and carefully searched the dead man's pockets, extracting a set of car keys from the right hand trouser pocket.

"Has he been identified yet?" he asked, straightening up.

"The school caretaker says his name is Atherly and that he used to be a master here."

"Was the caretaker the person who found the body?"

"Yes, he and one of the masters; though actually it was first discovered by the head-master's wife."

Yule's nose twitched with interest, while

the officer went on to explain. He seldom interrupted when being given the facts of a case and was apt to become testy when anyone did it to him.

"Let's go and have a look at the car," he said, when the officer had finished. He turned to a sergeant who was hovering in the background. "Somebody'll have to stay here all night to make sure the scene isn't disturbed. I don't want souvenir hunters clambering all over the place. Once all the supporting troops have done their stuff, the body can be removed to the mortuary. Meanwhile, you'd better arrange for the area to be screened off from prying eyes."

Yule and one of the patrol car officers reached the parked car and the DCI gave a short, satisfied grunt when he found that the keys fitted the door lock. Opening the driver's door, he peered inside.

"I don't want to search it thoroughly until it's been fingerprinted," he remarked. Then sticking his head farther in, he sniffed. "Unless I'm much mistaken, somebody's been smoking cannabis. What do you think?"

"I agree, sir," the officer said, withdrawing his head.

"Something else for the lab boys to examine."

He was about to close the car door when his eye was caught by something white on the floor beneath the driver's seat. He reached down and picked up a folded card. It had a lovers' knot of roses design on the front. Inside, in a clear, bold hand, was written:

"Same time, same place this week, my dearest."

It was dated simply "Sunday" and bore no signature. He peered around for an envelope, but didn't see one.

A few minutes later he got into his car to drive up to the school. It was early days yet, but he felt more cautiously optimistic than he usually did at that stage of an investigation.

It seemed to Yule that there were pale, eager faces pressed against every pane of glass of the upstairs windows. It was clear that nobody was asleep at Easter House School that night. The truth was that the boys were finding events more exciting than bonfire night and Christmas Eve put together. Moreover the dormitory area was pulsating with rumours. The headmaster had shot a burglar: the headmaster had shot his wife: his wife had shot him: the school had been uncovered as the headquarters of a master criminal . . . and so on. No suggestion was too lurid not to be worthy of further embellishment.

Yule met his first obstacle when, on announcing that he wished to see Mrs. Brigstock, he was informed that she was in bed and asleep, a doctor having given her a sedative and instructed that she was not to be disturbed.

"If I can't disturb her, then nobody else can," Yule said to the sergeant who had given him the information.

"I've seen to that, sir. I've got Woman Police Constable Whitaker sitting at her bedside."

They both knew that with Winnie Whitaker on duty, not even a herd of elephants would get past.

"What about Mr. Brigstock? Where's he?"

"In his study, sir. I'd describe him as being in a state of suppressed agitation."

"I take it then he's not under sedation?"

"No, sir. When I heard you were on your way, I said nobody was to question him before you arrived."

"When did he return?"

"Can't help on that, sir. One moment he was still absent, the next he was standing by the front door with a bewildered sort of look."

Just then a car pulled up outside and Detective Inspector Hart sprang out.

"Ah, the right man at the right moment," Yule remarked by way of greeting. "I was just about to interview the headmaster about the evening's events."

"From what I've heard, it sounds like a straightforward case," Trevor Hart said robustly.

"Time will tell," Yule replied.

Richard Brigstock was pacing up and down when the two officers entered his study. His head was held forward as though he was about to use it to assault somebody. He shook hands as Yule introduced himself and DI Hart.

"I'm at your service," he said stiffly, "though there's little I can tell you as I was out this evening. It was the monthly meeting of our local Natural History Society. We met at Lady Darton's home over at Wickenby."

"What time was the meeting?"

"Eight thirty."

"How long does it take you to drive there?"

"Normally about twenty-five minutes."

"What do you mean by normally?"

"In fact, I allowed extra time this evening as I wanted to stop and examine a new badger sett I'd heard about."

"So what time did you leave?"

"About a quarter to eight."

"Which means you spent about twenty minutes at the badger sett?"

"Rather longer. I lost sense of time and arrived late for the meeting. I didn't get there until about ten minutes to nine. Lady Darton can confirm that."

"More importantly, Mr. Brigstock, who can confirm what you were doing between a quarter to eight and ten minutes to nine?"

"I hope my own word is sufficient," the headmaster said austerely.

Yule was thoughtful for a moment, then

fixing Mr. Brigstock with a steady gaze he asked, "Do you own a shotgun?"

Brigstock started. "Yes; but you're not, I hope, suggesting I killed Atherly? I've had it for years and hold a police permit. You can check that at your own headquarters."

"Where do you keep it?"

"In that cupboard," he said, indicating a door in a corner of the room.

"I'd like to see it."

Brigstock rose and, without a word, went over and opened the cupboard door. It revealed a deep recess with shelves on either side which were stacked with files and papers. Propped against the far wall was a leather gun-case which he picked up and brought over to Yule.

"When did you last use it?" the DCI asked as he unbuckled the securing straps of the case.

"Last month. I was invited to a pheasant shoot by Colonel Fox. After-wards I cleaned it and put it away. I've not used it since."

Yule gave a nod which did no more than indicate he had heard what the headmaster said. Then, removing the gun from its case, he broke it and put his nose to the breech, while Brigstock watched him in wary silence. Returning the gun to its case with care, he handed it to DI Hart.

"The lab will need to examine it," he said. Turning to the headmaster he added, "Just routine, you understand?"

From Brigstock's expression it was clear that, even if he understood, he was anything but happy with the turn of events. It was with considerable bitterness that he said, "I hope you realise the effect all your probings are bound to have on my school. As if things haven't been difficult enough these past few weeks!"

"You mean, as a result of Jason Cutler's death?"

"Yes."

Yule let out a sigh. "I'm not here to make things worse for you, Mr. Brigstock, but I'm investigating a murder and if that means upsetting a few applecarts . . ." He gave a graphic shrug as he left the sentence unfinished. After a pause he went on, "When did you first learn that it was Atherly who'd been killed?"

"As soon as I returned. Mr. Winslow met me as I was putting the car away and told me what had happened. I realised, of course, that something was up because of all the cars outside."

"What time did you get back?"

"Less than half an hour ago. I paid a second visit to the badger sett on my way."

"Getting back to Atherly, I gather he was once a master here?"

"It was about two or three years ago, for a couple of terms."

"Why did he leave?"

"Because he was unsatisfactory," Brigstock said icily.

"In what way unsatisfactory?"

"In every way."

"Is it true that he paid court to your wife?"

"I don't wish to discuss that."

"Were you aware that he has continued seeing your wife since leaving the school?"

Brigstock hesitated a second before answering. "No," he said firmly.

"Is that your wife's handwriting?" Yule asked, suddenly producing the note he had found on the car floor.

The headmaster seemed to undergo a

psychedelic change of colour as he stared at the writing.

"Where did this come from?" he asked angrily.

Ignoring the question, Yule went on in the same quiet, dispassionate tone, "Have you spoken to your wife since you got back from your meeting?"

"I was told she was under sedation and mustn't be disturbed," he said with a touch of resentment.

"Who told you that?"

"Matron. She was passing on what the doctor had said."

"Do you have any idea what your wife was doing at the old summer-house between eight thirty and nine this evening?"

The headmaster glared as if one of his boys had just stuck out his tongue at him.

"She sometimes used to go out for a late breath of fresh air," he said bleakly. "I imagine she was passing the old summer-house and saw the body lying there. No wonder she arrived back in a state of shock."

Yule appeared to ponder this interpretation of events before he spoke again.

"On the evidence so far," he said at length, "it seems to me more likely that she went to the old summer-house and found him dead. Incidentally, I take it your wife would have known you'd be out this evening?" Brigstock gave a curt nod and Yule went on, "Of course, if you were aware your wife was still carrying on with Atherly, you'd have had a motive for killing him."

"That's a preposterous suggestion. In fact, it's a gross slander."

Unperturbed by the outburst, Yule went on, "I think that's all for the time being, Mr. Brigstock, but I'll certainly wish to interview you further after I've talked to your wife."

The two officers rose and departed, leaving the headmaster of Easter House School looking anxious and agitated.

"I reckon he's our man," Hart said as they walked away from the study. "He had both motive and opportunity. All that guff he gave us about visiting a badger's sett! What he was doing was committing a murder and covering his tracks. He obviously found out that his wife and the deceased had an assignation and lay in wait. I think we ought to take him in and see if a bit of brooding in a cell doesn't loosen his tongue."

"I'd like to hear the other side of the story first," Yule remarked.

"Which other side?"

"Mrs. Brigstock's. After all she had as good an opportunity and, who knows, as strong a motive to kill Atherly. Moreover, people who find dead bodies always have some explaining to do, so I'm not jumping to any conclusions yet."

It was two thirty before Yule got to bed; bed being in this instance a large, battered armchair in a corner of his office. He often slept there when he was on a serious case. The fact was that his own marriage had been a disastrous failure and should never have taken place. So much for hindsight. However, he and Beryl soon fell into going their own ways, though still bound together in the eyes of the law and, more important to his wife, those of the church. He dutifully supported her while she adamantly refused on religious grounds to consider a divorce. Fortunately, there were no children and he was grateful to have a job that kept him busy eighteen hours a day, and more if he wanted. The one thing he dreaded was retirement, but that was still several years off. For her part Beryl had never shown the slightest interest in his work and never questioned his absences from home. Though they still shared a bedroom, they had long since occupied separate beds with a healthy space between them. Given all this, it was no hardship to Yule to spend the night in his office chair wrapped in a blanket.

At six o'clock his phone rang and brought him out of a dreamless sleep.

"Thought I'd let you know, sir, that Mrs. Brigstock is awake and about to get dressed," WPC Whitaker announced.

"Thanks. I'll be over right away."

He was one of those fortunate people who could be fast asleep one moment and wide awake the next, without any intermediate stage of bleary-eyed yawning.

He re-knotted his tie, put on his shoes and jacket, combed his hair and was ready to leave. He could have done with a cup of tea, but that would have to wait. Three minutes later he was on his way.

He arrived to find a very different scene

from the previous night. Gone were all the faces at the upstairs windows; gone, too, all the cars, save one. He parked next to it and got out. He pictured the boys lying in exhausted slumber after all the excitement and thought it improbable that much work would be done in the classroom that day.

WPC Whitaker opened the front door as he approached.

"Heard your car, sir," she said, standing aside to let him enter. Though resembling an overblown blonde bombshell, she was a tough, resourceful officer, who had tackled many an obstreperous male and rather enjoyed putting her karate lessons into practice.

"Mrs. Brigstock's in the headmaster's drawing-room," she said. "I've told her you were on your way."

"How does she seem?"

"Composed, but a bit edgy."

"Has she made any reference to last night's events?"

"No and I haven't encouraged her to talk. I thought that was better left to you, sir."

Yule nodded. "Let's go and find her.

Incidentally, have you seen Mr. Brigstock this morning?"

"No. He spent the night in his study."

"That makes two of us," Yule reflected wryly. "He didn't make any attempt to see his wife?"

She shook her head. "Do I take it, sir, that he's our number one suspect?"

"I'll tell you after I've talked to his wife."

They arrived outside the drawing-room door, which WPC Whitaker opened with a flourish. It was a large room and was in darkness apart from a pool of light shed by a tall standard lamp. Sally Brigstock sat in a chair on the fringe of the lighted area, smoking a cigarette. She looked up as they entered, but made no attempt to move.

"I'm Detective Chief Inspector Yule, Mrs. Brigstock, and I'd like to ask you some questions about last night if you feel up to it." And even if you don't, he added to himself.

Sally Brigstock nodded. Turning to WPC Whitaker, she said, "Be a dear and fetch us some tea from the kitchen. They'll have begun getting the boys' breakfast, which means there'll be a large brown pot of tea sitting on the table. Just go in and help yourself. There's more tea drunk in this place in the course of a day than beer at a German beer festival."

WPC Whitaker departed on her errand after receiving a green light from Yule. He, meanwhile, pulled up a hardback chair and positioned it at right angles to where Sally Brigstock was sitting.

"Why don't you begin by telling me about last night and then I'll ask you any questions I think necessary?"

She gave a small pout. "What more is there to tell?"

"A great deal more. For a start, I want to hear your version of events."

"I don't have a version. You make it sound as if I've concocted a story."

"I didn't mean to do that," Yule said patiently.

"I suppose you've already spoken to Peter Winslow?"

"Yes."

"And to my husband?" Yule nodded and she went on, "I wonder what he told you? I suppose you won't say."

"As you know, your husband attended a meeting last night—"

"So he says!"

Yule gave her a sharp look. "Would you care to explain that remark?"

At that moment WPC Whitaker returned bearing a tray with three mugs of tea on it. After handing them round, she sat down and pulled out her notebook.

"Well, Mrs. Brigstock?" Yule said. "What exactly did you mean?"

"Have you confirmed that my husband was at the meeting?"

"Do you have any reason to doubt it?"

"I don't know what he's told you, do I? All I do know is that he left home earlier than he usually does. Perhaps you should ask him why?"

"At the moment I'm more interested in getting facts from you. For instance, what were you doing in the vicinity of the old summer-house around eight thirty to nine last night?"

"I'd gone for a walk. I often do. Anyone can tell you that."

"It seems an unlikely walk to take on a damp November evening."

"Not at all unlikely. I was on school property the whole time."

"But crossing rough fields in the dark . . ."

"Why not?" she broke in. "Anyway, I'm not afraid of the dark and it's a walk I know." Her tone was querulous.

"What caused you to glance inside the summer-house when you got there?"

"It was a perfectly natural thing to do."

Why was she behaving like a petulant adolescent, Yule wondered? Was it a cover for inner turmoil or was it a bit of natural self being manifested?

"Anyway, what did you see when you looked inside?" he asked.

"I saw the body."

"Yes?"

She gave a small convulsive shudder and hid her face in her hands.

"It was the most horrible sight I've ever seen," she said in a tremulous voice.

"Did you recognise the person?" She shook her head vigorously. "But you know now who it was?" She nodded. Her truculence had seemingly evaporated and Yule went on, "Philip Atherly used to be a master here, didn't he? Were you surprised when you learnt he was the dead person?"

"I was shattered."

"You'd kept in touch with him after he'd left the school, had you not?"

"I may have seen him once or twice."

"You were lovers, weren't you?"

"Who says so?"

"Answer my question."

She threw him a sidelong look of hatred.

"I'm a married woman," she said, with a sudden muster of dignity, "and I have a position to maintain."

"Are you happily married?"

"What a silly question!"

"Your husband's more than twenty years older than yourself, yes?" Yule went on with a quiet relentlessness.

"If you say so."

It struck Yule that she had quickly regained control of her emotions. He wondered if she was mildly schizophrenic with such sudden changes of mood. It was time to play his trump card.

"Is that your handwriting, Mrs. Brigstock?" he asked, showing her the card he had found on the floor of the car.

She stared at it as though mesmerised, then turned her head away. After a pause she said, "Yes, all right, it is my writing. So what of it?"

"Did you send it to Philip Atherly?"

"Yes."

"And did it refer to meeting him in the old summer-house last night?"

"Yes."

"But when you got there, he was dead?"

"Yes, except that I didn't recognise him at first . . ." Her voice trailed away.

"Have you any idea who might have killed him?"

"Does everything have to be spelt out? Of course, I have an idea. So must you if you can add two and two together and make four."

"You believe it was your husband?"

"Who else?"

"You, Mrs. Brigstock. You had the opportunity and it's not hard to envisage a motive."

9

OVER the next two days, Rosa scoured the papers for further news of Philip Atherly's death. All she learnt, however, was that police enquiries were continuing. She presumed there was still some link missing in the evidence against Richard Brigstock, headmaster and avenging husband. She wasn't to know that the officer in charge of the case was not one to rush his fences.

Come Friday and a promising weather forecast for the weekend, she decided she would drive down to Sussex on Saturday and see what she could find out. She wished that Peter Chen were back as he was invaluable on the sort of expedition she had in mind, not only as a companion, but as an enthusiastic ally in digging out information.

Having made up her mind to go, she immediately suffered cold feet. What was she supposed to do when she got there? It was a question that had been recurring in her mind ever since Charlotte's visit.

She could understand that somebody as apparently feckless and insensitive as Philip Atherly might have accepted the risks of stoking up the jealousy of an outraged husband, but what could she reasonably do when he met an end he had partially foreseen? It was more than puzzling.

She also still scanned the papers for further news of Trina Forbes. Her mind's-eye picture of the girl sitting opposite her in the train had never faded.

It was just as she was about to leave the office on Friday evening that Stephanie announced that Inspector Gainham was on the phone.

"Put him through, Steph," she said, eager to hear what he had to say.

"Miss Epton? I don't know whether you saw a piece in the paper last week about Katrina Forbes having been in touch with her parents?"

"Yes, I did. Has there been further news?"

"She phoned her mother two days ago

98

and told her not to worry as she was all right."

"Did she say where she was calling from?"

"No. Her previous contact, you may remember, was a letter with a London postmark, but this time she was phoning from abroad. She didn't mention where, but from something she said, her mother deduced she was in a country on a different timescale."

"America, perhaps?"

"No, the other direction. It was around ten o'clock when her call came through, but in the course of their short conversation, Trina let slip that it was almost midnight where she was. Apparently it wasn't a very good line and at one point the operator broke in in what Mrs. Forbes describes as pidgin English."

"But otherwise no clue as to her whereabouts?"

"None."

"Well, at least she's still alive, even if her disappearance remains shrouded in mystery."

"Anyway, I thought I'd let you know, Miss Epton, in view of your interest.

There's obviously nothing more the police can do in the circumstances."

"No, I can see that. But thank you all the same for keeping me informed."

"Her behaviour's a total enigma," Inspector Gainham observed in a tone that boded ill for Trina Forbes should they ever come face to face.

Rosa could only agree.

The caprices of English weather can require you to wear thermal underwear in June and let you bask in the sun in November.

The next day, Saturday, was just such a day, with the sun shining out of a clear blue sky as Rosa drove her small Honda car out of London. Two hours later she arrived in the village of Oakway. As she approached she saw a sign, inscribed "Easter House School", pointing up a long, tree-lined drive and she stopped the car to have a better look. The school was clearly visible about four hundred yards away, with playing fields lying in between.

After a few minutes she drove on until she reached an intersection, when it suddenly occurred to her that this must be the spot where Jason Cutler had met his death.

Parking the car on the grass verge at the side of the road, she got out and peered over the hedge. One corner of the school could still be seen, but the main bulk of the building was hidden by a crescent of trees. Presumably it was somewhere here that Jason had scrambled through the hedge, across the verge and into the path of the car that killed him. She walked on a few yards and found a place where the hedge's growth was stunted, making it a negotiable obstacle. It was just short of the intersection of two narrow roads, along one of which Rosa had travelled after turning off the main road a mile and a half farther back.

As she continued to gaze over the hedge, her eye was caught by a wooden structure to her right. It was close to the apex of the field and melted into the background of grey-trunked poplar trees which lined the road on that flank. There was a length of white marking tape dangling from a branch and Rosa realised she was looking at the old summer-house.

The police had obviously cordoned it off

with tape, a length of which had subsequently got caught up in the tree.

She wondered whether to clamber through the hedge and take a closer look. She couldn't see anybody about and decided to do so.

Hugging the hedge so that she approached along two sides of a triangle, she reached the summer-house and peered inside. Apart from the obvious signs of police examination, there was little to arouse her interest, though she found herself staring with morbid fascination at the chalk outline on the floor indicating where the body had lain.

She now knew where Jason Cutler and Philip Atherly had come by their respective deaths. So proximate and yet apparently without connection.

She returned to her car and decided to drive into Oakway which was half a mile on. She knew it had a pub called the Pheasant and resolved to make that her next port of call.

She spotted it as she was entering the village and found the car park almost empty. It was just after midday and there was no apparent surge of customers. It'd almost certainly be different in an hour's time.

There were no more than half a dozen people in the main bar and they all gave the impression of being habitués. A military-looking man was deep in conversation at one end of the bar with someone whom Rosa assumed to be the publican. A pleasant-faced redhead was polishing glasses at the other end and Rosa approached her. The woman gave her a smile.

"Yes, dear, what can I get you?"

"A lager and lime, please. A small one. And I'd also like something to eat."

The woman pointed at a blackboard at the end of the counter on which the day's menu was written in smudged chalk.

"Cornbeef hash sounds good," she said. "Do you do the cooking yourself?"

"No. Dolly comes in every morning and does it. But I can guarantee you'll enjoy it. She's the best cook in the village." As she got Rosa her drink, she went on, "Haven't seen you in here before, have I?"

"No, I've just driven down from London." Rosa gave her a smile. "If I'm right, that's where you come from?"

103

"Jim and I'll never pass for locals," the woman remarked cheerfully. "We came here from Bethnal Green about seven years ago, but we're still foreigners." Nodding in the direction of the man talking at the farther end of the bar, she added, "That's my husband, Jim. I'm Gina." She gave Rosa a quizzical look. "I take it you're not just down for the scenery?"

Rosa blushed slightly. "No, I'm not. At least, I'm combining a day in the country with a bit of information-seeking. I'm a solicitor."

"A solicitor, eh?" Gina observed with the alertness of a magpie that's suddenly spotted something bright under a hedgerow. "Would you be having anything to do with all our goings-on?"

"The murder, you mean?"

"Or the death of that poor little lad from the school?"

"All I know about either is what I've read in the papers," Rosa said, deciding not to reveal her connection with Philip Atherly. "Somebody I know was a friend of the murdered man and is terribly upset by what's happened."

"He doesn't have many mourners in

these parts," Gina remarked with a touch of lemon in her tone. "As you may know he used to teach up at the school. He wasn't a very popular figure in the village."

"What did he do?"

"He borrowed money from my husband and made off without repaying it, but that was a relatively small matter in his catalogue of nastiness. You see the man Jim's talking to?" Rosa nodded. "That's Colonel Fox. He's a wealthy landowner in this area. Atherly seduced his sixteen-year-old daughter, so that she had to have an abortion. As you can imagine that didn't endear him to the Colonel. And then we later heard how he was carrying on all the while with Mrs. Brigstock. She's the headmaster's wife at Easter House School and a good twenty years younger than her husband. I reckon he cleared off just in time. His mistake was to come back again . . ."

"How do you mean?"

"Rumour has it that he and Mrs. Brigstock have gone on seeing one another." She paused and gave Rosa a wry look. "Some folk never learn, do they?"

"I gather nobody's yet been arrested for the murder."

"It's only a matter of time. Obviously Mr. Brigstock found out what was going on . . . If there's any justice he'll get a light sentence. After all, he was provoked."

"Presumably the police are still looking for evidence."

"As I say, it's just a matter of time. After all, who else could have done it?"

It seemed to Rosa that, from what Gina had told her, the two men talking at the other end of the bar fitted the bill. It might, however, have been less than tactful to say so.

"And the boy who was run down and killed, that still appears to be an unsolved mystery," she remarked in a speculative tone.

She became aware that Gina was looking past her towards the door and turned to see what had attracted her attention. A young man had just come in and was staring towards the other end of the bar where Colonel Fox and Gina's husband were still talking. It was as if he were hoping to attract the landlord's attention, but when he failed to do so, he came up to the bar close to where Rosa was perched on a stool. He had a strained, exhausted look, but gave Gina a wan smile.

"Your usual?" she enquired.

He nodded and watched her as she drew half a pint of lager.

"Who's the man Jim's talking to?" he asked.

"Colonel Fox."

"Ah!"

"We were just talking about your poor little brother," Gina said. "This lady's a solicitor from London." Turning to Rosa, she added, "This is Jason Cutler's brother." Then turning back to Cutler she went on, "You look as if you could do with a bit of cheering up. I'll go and put on that tape of The Stance, I know they're your favourite group."

Rosa felt somewhat nonplussed by the turn the conversation had taken, but realised that it was up to her to explain her presence to the new arrival.

Toby Cutler, meanwhile, was staring at her with a mixture of curiosity and suspicion. Apart from his washed-out appearance, he was, Rosa decided, a good-looking young man, with fair hair and regular features. She didn't imagine he had any problem finding girl-friends, though she thought she could detect a certain petulance in his manner.

"I first read about your brother's death in the paper when I was visiting a client in Lewes prison," she now said. "It's haunted me ever since, so I can imagine what an effect it must have had on you and everyone who knew him. By the way, my name's Rosa Epton."

"And you're a solicitor?"

"Yes, but I'm not here on official business today," Rosa said, with a disarming smile. It was close enough to the truth.

"I suppose you've also heard about the murder? Somebody shot in the grounds of Easter House School."

"That sounds an altogether more straightforward affair."

"Perhaps it is, perhaps it isn't."

"Doesn't anyone have an idea what your brother was doing out of his dormitory that night?"

"I don't personally believe he was

running away. He'd always seemed perfectly happy there."

"Then what?"

"Jason was a bit of a romantic. I don't mean he had a girl-friend. But he enjoyed adventure stories and liked identifying himself with their heroes. It's possible he was living out something he'd read or seen on TV."

"And was mown down by a hit-and-run driver?" Rosa said a trifle incredulously.

"I'm not suggesting he was deliberately dicing with death."

"No, that would be too bizarre. Is it possible he'd gone to meet someone?"

Toby Cutler frowned. "I think the head-master believes that, but I don't. I don't know if you're familiar with the place where it happened. Two narrow, twisting lanes intersect and the driver wouldn't have expected to find a kid wandering in the road at that hour. He was probably whizzing along too fast for safety and . . ." He completed the sentence with a graphic shrug.

It sounded to Rosa almost as if he was exonerating the driver and she said so.

"Far from it," he retorted. "He killed my brother and didn't stop and that was unforgivable."

"I imagine the police have tried to trace the damaged car?"

"And drawn a blank." He pulled a face. "They certainly gave my car a thorough going-over. I had to account for every dent and scratch."

"Is it possible that this person who's just been murdered knew your brother?"

"He'd ceased to be a master at the school before Jason arrived, so I don't see how he could have known him."

"If Atherly was still seeing Mrs. Brigstock, as I gather was the case, might your brother have been used as a go-between? A sort of messenger, if, for example, Mrs. Brigstock was unable to get away for one of their assignations."

"That's a new one," Toby Cutler said in a thoughtful voice. "Mrs. Brigstock would certainly have been capable of using Jason in the way you suggest. Incidentally, have you met her?" Rosa shook her head. "She's the sort of woman who'll make a pass at any male who's reached the age of puberty. A real nympho."

"Did Jason like her?"

"She was always very sweet to him and he appreciated that."

"And if, as you say, he had this romantic hero streak, he'd have been rather thrilled to undertake secret missions for the headmaster's wife," Rosa said, warming to her theme.

"If you're right, Atherly was probably the driver of the car that killed Jason."

"It doesn't necessarily follow. It could have been another car some way ahead of Atherly's."

"In which event, why didn't he stop when he found Jason lying dead at the roadside?"

"He may well have done so, but realising there was nothing he could do, he drove on. After all, he wouldn't have wanted to explain what he was doing there."

Rosa paused and reviewed the argument she had just propounded. If it contained a flaw, she couldn't see it, but was its premise a sound one? That was something only Jason Cutler could have said for certain.

From all she had heard, one thing

emerged very clearly, namely that Philip Atherly had been more adept at making enemies than friends. Not that this came as a great surprise.

10

THREE years on and Joanna Fox still carried the scars of what had happened. It wasn't so much the discovery that she was pregnant as a result of her brief fling with Philip Atherly, as her father's insistence on an abortion that had left her emotionally in shreds.

The abortion, carried out in an expensive private clinic, had been followed by a mental breakdown which had necessitated further expensive treatment in another private clinic.

Now just twenty, she had outwardly recovered in that she had a job in London and lived during the week with an aunt who had a flat in Knightsbridge. For the past eighteen months she had worked as a research assistant to a partially crippled writer who was a friend of her aunt. She enjoyed the job which involved her spending hour upon hour in the timeless atmosphere of libraries. Its great attraction, from her point of view, was that she worked on her own and wasn't required to mix with other people, for the unhappy truth was that she was still neurotic about facing the world, and men in particular. She had no boy-friends and it looked as if her first sexual experience could also be her last.

She normally returned to Oakway at weekends, when her father would meet her on Friday evenings at the mainline station about six miles from the village.

Though she spent most of her days reading and making notes for her employer, she seldom looked at a newspaper. Thus she was unaware of Atherly's death until the weekend that followed it.

Colonel Fox and his wife had both been in their mid-thirties when they got married and Joanna had not been born for a further three years, so that she found herself the only child of older than usual parents. Mrs. Fox had developed hypochondria shortly after her daughter's birth and became convinced she had a weak heart. Neither doctors nor any number of cardiograms could persuade her otherwise. Her days were spent resting and looking out of the window, with sorties into the garden when the weather was right and she could sit in the sun with a rug over her knees.

"How's Mummy?" Joanna enquired dutifully as she got into the car at the station that Friday evening, being the day before Rosa's visit to the Pheasant.

"She's all right," her father replied brusquely, as he always did. Then as he manoeuvred the car out into the road he said, "There's been a murder in the village."

"A murder? In Oakway?"

"In the grounds of Easter House School."

Something warned her that this was more than an item of idle conversation.

"Who was murdered?" she asked warily.

"Atherly."

For a while she said nothing as she stared out at a row of well-lit shop windows.

"Has anyone been arrested?" she asked at length, still staring out of the car.

"No. Atherly's demise is no loss to society. He deserved extermination."

Joanna said nothing, but recalled the threats her father had uttered against the man who had seduced his daughter. It seemed unlikely, however, that he would have carried them out so long after the event, even though she knew him to be an implacable enemy and at times totally unforgiving. Moreover, he was fond of espousing the virtues of private justice over the uncertainties of that dispensed by the courts in circumstances which affected himself.

She became aware that her father was giving her a sidelong glance as she sat staring straight ahead. She found that she had no feelings at all about Philip Atherly's death. That episode in her life was like a paralysed limb. There was no longer any pain, though one was constantly reminded of its existence.

"What are you thinking?" he asked abruptly as they reached the main road out of the town.

"I was wondering who could have killed him," she replied.

"I could have, for one," he remarked with a short bark of a laugh.

"And did you?"

"I'd hardly be likely to admit it if I had, would I?"

"I don't know." After a pause she said, "Are there any rumours as to who did it?"

"Brigstock, the headmaster at Easter House School, seems to be the prime suspect."

"Surely not."

"Why do you say that?"

"Headmasters don't murder people."

"That's a very naïve remark. Given the right combination of circumstances, there isn't anyone who couldn't commit a murder. Anyway, I gather that Brigstock had both motive and opportunity. He's a prissy sort of fellow. Perhaps headmasters need to be. I've asked him over to shoot once or twice when I've been short of numbers."

"How was the murder committed?"

"He was shot. At close range." He paused. "I thought it best to tell you before we got to the house. Wasn't too sure how you'd react. But you don't seem too affected."

"What's Mummy's reaction?"

"Oh, it requires more than somebody's sudden death to take her mind off herself."

It was the next day when her father had

gone off to the Pheasant for a midday drink and her mother was resting upstairs that Joanna decided to do some investigating.

There was a high, shallow cupboard that ran along one of the walls in his study. In it he kept his sporting tackle, four shot-guns and a number of fishing rods. The guns, two twelve-bore double-barrel Purdeys and two single-barrel of similar quality, were in a built-in rack at one end of the cupboard. Above was a shelf with boxes of cartridges and cleaning materials. Although the cupboard was kept locked, Joanna knew where to find the key.

She didn't seriously believe her father had killed Philip Atherly, but there was a certain ambivalence about his attitude that aroused her curiosity.

Although the house was empty apart from her mother upstairs, she tiptoed into the study and closed the door quietly behind her. She found the key in its customary hiding-place and went across to unlock the cupboard. A quick glance told her that all four guns were in their place.

She wasn't sure what she had expected to find and suddenly felt rather foolish,

118

standing like an uneasy burglar in her father's study.

The twin-barrel guns were the ones he always used for shooting, the other two being seldom taken from their rack. On an impulse she put out a hand and ran a finger down the nearest single-barrel gun. She could tell in an instant that it had been recently oiled, whereas when she did the same thing to its companion her finger became coated with a fine film of oil mixed with dust.

She stood back and thought. There was only one logical explanation, the freshly oiled gun had been recently used and cleaned.

To what purpose, she wondered? She knew there could be a perfectly innocent explanation. On the other hand . . .

Detective Chief Inspector Yule was determined to await the result of the scientific examination of various items before deciding whether to charge Richard Brigstock with murder. In particular, he wanted to hear what a firearms expert had to say about the headmaster's shotgun.

Was there evidence that it had been recently fired? That was the vital question.

In the view of the doctor who had conducted the autopsy, the gun that caused Atherly's death had been fired directly into his face at a range of two to three feet. The pellets had had little time to spread before finding their target, hence his appalling injuries. It had been a far messier death than would have been caused by a single bullet.

DI Hart was all for arresting the head-master and, as he put it, shaking a confession out of him at the station. But Yule refused to budge, even when summoned to headquarters to report on his enquiries.

"I agree, sir, that Brigstock had both opportunity and motive," he said to the Assistant Chief Constable, "but that's not proof he did it. Moreover, one has to bear in mind that his wife, whatever her feelings in the matter, can't be called as a prosecution witness. Even if she could be, I'm not at all sure that she wouldn't hedge her bets when it came to giving evidence against her husband. Her statement's equivocal, to say the least."

The ACC sighed. "Who else could have done it?" he asked with a touch of exasperation.

"In my view, sir, Mrs. Brigstock herself isn't entirely in the clear. We'll probably never know for certain what stage her relationship with Atherly had reached. Supposing he'd driven down to tell her at their meeting he wanted to end their association?"

"She'd hardly have gone armed with a shotgun unless she had an inkling of what he was going to say."

"I agree, sir, but who knows whether or not she did? She's certainly not going to admit it. It'd be tantamount to handing us a motive." The ACC sighed again, rather more heavily, and Yule went on, "In my view, sir, it would be irresponsible to charge a man in Brigstock's position without a cast-iron case. The consequences would be disastrous for his school. It may come to that, but surely we need to be ccrtain before we make a move."

"You're almost suggesting there's one law for the rich and one for the poor. One for headmasters and one for lesser mortals."

Yule looked at the ACC with mild surprise. "I thought we both knew it was so in practice, sir. Once the evidence is there, I agree that the suspect's status is irrelevant, but, in my experience, we've always moved more cautiously where a suspect is someone of position."

It was not a line of argument the ACC was inclined to take up. Instead, after a third sigh he said, "I suppose, anyway, Brigstock is unlikely to abscond."

"Extremely unlikely, sir."

"I hope that's right, for all our sakes."

It was following his meeting with the Assistant Chief Constable that Yule decided it might be useful to compare notes with Sergeant Richards. It so happened both of them were on duty that Sunday, which presented a good opportunity.

"Has it occurred to you, Sergeant, that our two cases could be connected?" Yule said when they were sitting in his office.

"It's certainly struck me as a coincidence that Jason Cutler and Atherly met their deaths within fifty yards of one another."

Yule frowned. "You're not suggesting it was planned that way?"

"I can't see how it could have been, sir, but it's a remarkable coincidence."

Yule was thoughtful for a while. "How does this strike you?" he asked and went on to propound the same theory Rosa had advanced the previous day when she met Toby Cutler. Namely that Jason Cutler had been used as a message bearer between Sally Brigstock and her lover.

Richards nodded slowly as he absorbed the implications. "It would explain the letter we found in young Cutler's locker, sir. 'Keep up the good work' could obviously have referred to his role as a go-between and the £5 note was a reward for services rendered."

"It fits quite neatly," Yule said in a reflective tone.

"Though it still doesn't explain, sir, how Jason Cutler came to be run down."

"Perhaps the obvious answer is the correct one, namely that it was a hit-and-run driver who had no connection with young Cutler or anyone else and has simply been able to vanish in the crowd. It's always those without any apparent connection with a crime who are the hardest to trace. The murderer who was unknown to his victim, the hit-and-run driver on a lonely road, they're the ones who are often never found."

It sounded plausible enough and yet Sergeant Richards had his doubts. Would the headmaster's wife have used one of the school's pupils quite so shamelessly, not to say recklessly? It would have needed only one word from the boy to someone in authority to have created a scandal of reverberating proportions.

And if Jason Cutler hadn't been a messenger, the original question hung in the air as large as ever. What had he been doing out of his dormitory that evening?

After working through the weekend, Monday failed to strike the sort of dread in Yule's heart that it managed to induce in most people going back to work after a leisured weekend.

He had actually gone home for a few hours' sleep on Sunday night, but was back in his office by eight o'clock the next morning.

Later he went out to interview a farmhand who lived in a cottage not far from the school and who was a renowned poacher in the area. When interviewed the day after the murder, he said he knew nothing that could help the police, but Yule decided to go and see him himself. If he'd been out on the evening in question, it was possible he had seen or heard something that could be pieced into the puzzle. The enquiry had already reached the stage of re-interviewing potential witnesses in the hope of jogging their memories.

On this occasion, however, Yule's journey proved fruitless as the man was having a day off and had gone into Lewes. He hadn't long returned to the station when Detective Constable Illingworth, who was the scene-of-crime officer in the case, burst into his room.

"I've just had the lab on the phone, sir. They've examined the shotgun and say it hadn't been fired for several weeks."

"How can they be so certain?" Yule asked in a faintly nettled tone.

"They found a small spider in the barrel, which appeared to have had its home there for some time."

"Oh!" Yule said bleakly, his hopes

dashed by a tiny industrious creature no larger than a breadcrumb.

"But there is something else, sir," Illingworth went on. "They've found a blood smear on the instep of Brigstock's left shoe, which matches the deceased's blood group."

"And that's different from Brigstock's own group," Yule observed with quiet satisfaction.

"Exactly, sir."

Yule recalled how reluctant the headmaster had been when asked to provide a blood sample and to hand over various items of his clothing for scientific examination. He had blustered and waxed indignant, and been only partially mollified when assured it was purely a matter of routine.

He must know he was a suspect, the DCI reflected, and yet he had behaved throughout as if this were unthinkable. Well, he now had something further to explain.

The time had come for a full-scale interrogation.

11

MR. BRIGSTOCK had just finished a Latin lesson with the top form when Yule and Hart drove up to the front entrance. The classroom looked out at the back so that he didn't see their arrival.

The boys released from following Hannibal's journey across the Alps with his vast army of men, horses and elephants were putting away their books and waiting for the headmaster to leave before letting off a bit of steam and turning their attention to French. For most, anything was a relief after Latin.

"There are two men waiting in your study, sir," Fred, the handyman, said as Brigstock emerged from the classroom.

His expression, always somewhat austere, became more so.

"Who are they?" he asked, though he thought he knew the answer.

"Two police officers."

"How long have they been here?"

"They've only just arrived."

"They haven't spoken to anyone else?"

"No, sir."

"Is my wife in?"

"She went out in her car about forty minutes ago."

"Thank you."

His study lay at the end of a passage and was reached via a small lobby which had an outer door. This was normally kept open and closed only when the headmaster didn't wish to be disturbed. He now shut it firmly behind him and entered his study.

The two officers were standing together staring out of the window and turned on hearing the door open.

"I said we'd probably wish to see you again," Yule said, while DI Hart remained stony-faced. "I'd like you to accompany us to the police station. The car's outside."

"Are you arresting me?" Brigstock asked in a tense voice.

"I didn't use that word, did I?"

"What if I won't come?"

Yule sighed. "I'm sure you don't want to have the school's routine disrupted more than necessary. I'm offering you the easy option, but there are others."

"How long will this take?"

"I can't say. It depends . . ." Aware that DI Hart was showing signs of restiveness, he said, "So if you're ready, we'll go."

Brigstock stood as though cemented to the floor, gazing around his study as if he might never see it again.

"I'll have to let my deputy know I'm going out," he said at length.

"By all means. Can you speak to him on the internal phone?"

"I'll try."

"If not, you'll have to leave him a message."

Five minutes later, with Yule and the headmaster in the back of the car and DI Hart driving, they were on their way. Yule let out a quiet sigh of relief. He'd expected greater resistance, coupled with demands for a lawyer. Presumably Brigstock was hoping that by complying with a minimum of fuss, there was less likely to be a damaging showdown. As it was, nobody had seen their departure and he could hope to be back without the boys finding out where he had been.

As soon as they arrived at the station,

Yule led the way up to his office, which was not only functional, but shabby as well.

"Not as comfortable as a headmaster's study, I'm afraid," he remarked, as he waved Brigstock to the battered armchair in which he had so often spent the night.

At times such as this it was more a mantrap than a chair and gave the interrogating officer a distinct psychological advantage over its occupant.

"When I spoke to you on the night of the murder," Yule went on, "you told me you'd left home about seven forty-five to drive to Wickenby for a meeting which wasn't due to start till eight thirty—"

"I explained that," Brigstock broke in.

"As I was going to say before you interrupted, you left home early in order to examine a badger sett on your way and in the event didn't arrive at Lady Darton's house until a quarter to nine."

"I told you, I spent longer at the badger sett than I'd intended."

"I remember very clearly what you told me," Yule said with a touch of asperity. "The point is that a journey which normally takes only twenty-five minutes occupied a good hour on this occasion."

"I don't deny it."

"Did you stop anywhere else on the way, apart from the badger sett?"

"Do you have a particular reason for asking that?" Brigstock's tone was suspicious.

"I'd like an answer to my question."

"I'm entitled to know the reason for the question."

"Because you think it might be a trick question? Is that why you're reluctant to answer it?"

"I believe trick questions are not unknown to the police."

"Do you teach your boys to prevaricate, Mr. Brigstock?"

"That's an offensive remark."

"But justified in the circumstances."

There was a pause before the headmaster spoke again. Then he said, "The answer to your question is that I have no recollection of stopping anywhere else."

"You're quite sure of that."

"I've said I have no recollection of doing so."

"I don't know how you run a school if

your memory's that pathetic," Hart said with a sneer.

Brigstock gave him an angry glare which he subsequently directed at the apparatus on Yule's desk that was recording everything said, as well as each pregnant pause.

"Is that your considered reply," Yule said, "that you have no recollection of stopping anywhere else?"

"Yes."

"You remember quite clearly that you stopped at the badger sett?"

"I've said so."

"So that if you had made another stop, you'd be likely to recall it?"

Brigstock swallowed hard and fixed Yule with a searching look, as if trying to divine whether the DCI held a trump card which he was waiting to play. He appeared to see danger all around him, but Yule showed no inclination to offer him a helping hand.

"I remember now," he said stiffly, "I stopped to urinate just before I reached Lady Darton's."

"Where?"

"About half a mile from the house. I didn't wish to arrive and immediately absent myself to go to the cloakroom."

"So you got out of the car and had a pee at the side of the road?"

"Yes. There was nobody about."

"And you've suddenly remembered that?"

Brigstock nodded. "I'm sure you'll agree it's not the sort of event that sticks in the mind."

"Not like the scene of a murder, for example?"

Brigstock's expression became a mask. "I don't understand what you mean," he said with a tremor in his voice.

"Perhaps you can explain how one of your shoes has a blood smear on it which matches the deceased's blood?"

Watching him, Yule was reminded of a beetle lying on its back with legs waving furiously as it sought to turn over. But just as a beetle can right itself, so the headmaster's mental faculties reasserted themselves.

"There could be several reasons," he said in a shaky voice, "assuming what you say is true."

"It's what the lab says," Yule replied firmly. "Personally, I can think of only one reason, namely that, at some stage, you were present at the scene of Atherly's murder."

Yule had phrased his comment artfully, believing he was more likely to get an admission if he refrained from a direct accusation of murder.

"All I can think of is that my wife must have brought blood into the house after she'd discovered the body and that I picked some up on my shoes when I got back."

"Where, for example?"

"I've no idea."

"You've no idea because it's too far-fetched to be plausible," Hart broke in. "In any event by the time you returned, all the blood would have congealed, even in the old summer-house, which looked like an abattoir. The only place you could have picked up blood on your shoes was there at the time the murder was committed."

"Or shortly afterwards," Yule added in a voice that would have flattered a siren luring a boatload of sailors on to the rocks.

If they could get him to admit his presence at the scene of the murder, Yule would be more than satisfied. A case for prosecution was, more often than not, made up of dozens of small pieces.

Abruptly, without any warning, Brigstock leaned forward and buried his head in his hands. He remained so for a full minute. Then, slowly dropping his hands on to the arms of the chair, he said in a dulled tone, "Yes, all right, I did go to the old summer-house that evening. I'd seen a car parked in the lane nearby. . . ."

"What time was this?"

"Shortly after leaving home."

"You say that you saw a car parked in the lane, did you know whose it was?"

Brigstock hesitated. "No. But we've had people using the old summer-house and I was suspicious. Youths from the village have been going there and making an awful mess. It's been a nuisance rather than a problem, so I thought I'd go and investigate."

"What did you find?"

Again Brigstock hesitated, like a man picking his way through a minefield.

"I didn't find anything. You see, I never actually went inside."

"You'd better explain."

"From where I stood I could tell there

wasn't anyone inside so I didn't go any nearer."

"How close were you?"

"About twenty feet. There was no moon and the interior of the summer-house was totally dark."

"Then how do you know there was nobody there?"

"Because there weren't any sounds."

"What you're saying is that if there was a dead body lying on the floor, you wouldn't have seen it from where you stood."

"Exactly."

"So how do you account for the blood on your shoe?"

"I can only think that whoever killed Atherly must have carried blood away on his own shoes and contaminated the surrounding area."

If Brigstock was telling the truth, which Yule, anyway, doubted, it meant that the murder had been committed almost an hour before his wife discovered the body in the course of her evening walk. That is, if she'd told the truth, which Yule also doubted. In effect Brigstock was exculpating both of them, though almost certainly in his own rather than his wife's interest.

"Why didn't you tell me this when I first asked you about your movements?" Yule asked. "Why all the prevarication about not recalling stopping anywhere other than at the badger sett?"

Brigstock wriggled in the clutches of the battered chair.

"Put yourself in my shoes," he said. "Once I discovered there'd been a murder committed in the summer-house, it was the last place I could admit to visiting. You'd immediately connect me with the crime, even though I was totally ignorant of what had happened until I reached home that evening."

"What you're saying is that if the lab hadn't found blood on your shoe, you'd never have admitted your presence at the scene?"

Brigstock gave a resigned shrug. "My conscience was clear. Admitting I'd been close to the scene wasn't going to help you solve the crime. It would only add to my own troubles."

"What troubles?" DI Hart demanded to know.

Brigstock looked at him in surprise. "Surely that's obvious! First the mystery that still surrounds Jason Cutler's death and now somebody shot dead in a corner of the school grounds."

When, twenty minutes later, Yule brought the interview to an end and told the headmaster he would arrange for a car to take him home, DI Hart could no longer conceal his frustration.

"You had him hooked and let him wriggle away," he said in disgust.

"I agree his explanation about how the blood got on his shoe was a bit far-fetched, but it wasn't wholly implausible," Yule replied peaceably.

"It's obvious he'd found out about his wife's carryings-on and decided to put an end to Atherly's amorous capers."

"You believe he lay in wait for Atherly?"

"Either that or got to the summer-house ahead of his wife."

"What did he shoot him with?"

"We know that. A single-bore shotgun."

"But whose?"

138

Hart gave an impatient shrug to show his contempt for such pettifogging detail.

"Shotguns are two a penny in the country. Just because he didn't use the one we found in his cupboard doesn't mean he couldn't have got hold of another."

"If that's correct, I'd like to have evidence of it."

"So you're not proposing to charge him?" Hart said with a note of exasperation.

"Not yet. If the lab come up with something further, it could make all the difference." He gave the DI a faint smile. "Guns may go off at half-cock, I don't want to do the same."

12

FOLLOWING her visit to Oakway, Rosa spent Sunday catching up on domestic chores. As she swept, dusted and polished, she was still undecided whether to take on Philip Atherly's posthumous assignment.

It was true that her discussions in the Pheasant had further sharpened her interest in the curious events that had taken place; in particular she was puzzled by Toby Cutler's abrupt departure from the pub. He had suddenly broken off their conversation and gone. She'd at first thought he would reappear, that he'd beaten a hasty retreat to the loo, but when he failed to come back, she remarked to Gina on his behaviour.

"I know," Gina said. "I think he has moments of feeling suddenly overwhelmed by his brother's death and wants to go and hide himself. I'm sure it wasn't anything you said, dear."

It was shortly after this that Gina's

husband approached their end of the bar and his wife effected an introduction. By this time, however, the place was filling up and neither he nor his wife had any time for sustained conversation. Nevertheless, Rosa had the impression that the landlord was unduly interested in her presence.

During a lull in business, he returned to where she was finishing her meal.

"Are you Atherly's solicitor?" he asked.

"My interest in what's happened is personal rather than professional," she said, picking her words with care.

"I noticed you talking to Mr. Cutler; do you know him well?"

"I'd never met him before. I'd read about his brother's death in the paper."

"Looks more and more like the lad's death is connected in some way with the murder. Or rather the other way round. If you ask me, it was Atherly who sent the boy that letter with the £5 note."

Rosa looked mystified. "What letter?"

Jim Thesiger explained what he was referring to before he darted away to serve an influx of customers who had come in wearing particularly thirsty expressions.

As Rosa set about cleaning the bathroom

that Sunday morning, she pondered over what the landlord had told her. It seemed to support the theory she had advanced to Toby Cutler about his brother having served as a messenger between Philip Atherly and the headmaster's wife. What surprised her, however, was that Toby himself hadn't made any mention of the letter. Indeed, she recalled how he had at first rejected the idea that Atherly might have known his brother, though subsequently appeared to accept it as feasible.

Looking back now his omission seemed even stranger. Was the explanation that he knew more about events than he was prepared to admit? And that raised the further question, what had he to hide?

She finished her chores and made herself a cheese and pickle sandwich for lunch, which, together with a cup of black coffee, would sustain her until the evening when she was due to have supper with one of her married girl-friends whose husband was away in China on a business trip. Anthea, the friend in question, already had two children under the age of four and was heavily pregnant again.

"I just love babies," she was apt to say unnecessarily.

No wonder her husband was always off on business trips, Rosa reflected as she got ready to go out that evening. Though she was looking forward to seeing Anthea again after a longish interval, she wanted above all to talk to somebody about the matters that occupied her thoughts. And "somebody" meant either her partner, Robin, or Peter Chen. But Robin had been away from the office with a bad attack of 'flu for the past four days and Peter wasn't due back from his foreign travels until the next evening. He promised to call Rosa from Heathrow as soon as his plane arrived and she awaited his return with more than usual eagerness.

On Monday she was in court both morning and afternoon, the second occasion holding the fort for her ailing partner. When she got back to the office around four o'clock she prayed there wouldn't be a pile of paperwork requiring her attention. She knew the clerks would have done all they could, but inevitably there would be certain things only a partner could deal with.

She mounted the stairs to their first floor office and opened the reinforced oak door with its bronze plate bearing the inscription "Snaith and Epton, Solicitors".

Seated on a chair in the small reception area was Charlotte. Behind her, framed in the open hatch, Stephanie's face wore an expression of mute despair.

Before Charlotte could say anything, Stephanie spoke.

"I've already told this lady you'd be unlikely to see her without an appointment, but she insisted on waiting."

"I'm sorry to barge in like this," Charlotte said, standing up, "but I need to speak to you."

"Couldn't you have phoned? I'm particularly busy at the moment. I've been in court all day and my partner's away sick."

"I'm sorry," Charlotte said in a contrite voice, "but if I could just talk to you, I promise not to take up too much of your time."

"Very well," Rosa said with a sigh. "You'd better come along to my room." She turned to Stephanie. "I'm dying for a cup of tea, Steph, and I expect Miss Bailey could do with one, too."

She was rewarded with one of Stephanie's cool, sardonic glances that were her stock-in-trade.

"So what's happened?" Rosa asked when they reached her room and she had thrown her things down on a chair.

"Have you decided whether you'll take on the case?"

"I'm still uncertain what I'm supposed to take on." She paused. "As a matter of fact I drove down to Oakway on Saturday and mingled with the locals in the village pub."

"Did you find out anything?"

"Only that quite a few people had it in for Philip Atherly."

Charlotte nodded. "There were times when I felt like murdering him myself. He could be a selfish, egotistical male without even trying. I sometimes wonder why I put up with him for as long as I did. Probably because I also realised how vulnerable he was. He needed a girl-friend who was also a mother figure and I fitted the bill."

"I seem to recall his telling me that both his parents were dead."

"They were killed in a plane crash in India when Philip was sixteen. He was an only child and has no close relatives."

"I imagine he had a guardian after his parents' death?"

"An uncle whom he detested and who died three years ago."

Divested of family and short of friends, Philip Atherly had managed to get himself murdered. It seemed an inglorious end to an inglorious life. And yet Rosa remained sufficiently intrigued to want to know more about both; in particular his end.

"But none of this explains what brings you here today," Rosa said after a pause.

"The police have searched Philip's flat. I gather they were looking for drugs."

"Did they find any?"

"Some cannabis, but no hard stuff. They took away his address book."

"I suppose they're examining the possibility that his death was linked to some aspect of drug dealing. It's not unreasonable. After all, they'll have a record of his recent conviction. Will his address book have told them anything?"

"I've no idea. I knew he had one, though I've never seen it."

Rosa frowned as a thought occurred to her. "Did he leave a will?"

"That's what I've really come to see you about. He made one a few days after his court appearance."

"Do you know its contents?"

"I believe he's left everything, such as it is, to me. Apart, that is, from the money he specifically put aside to meet your charges."

"Do you happen to know where the will is?"

"I have it here," she said, reaching into a canvas shoulderbag she had placed on the floor beside her chair and producing a sealed envelope. "I've not opened it."

The envelope bore the bare inscription "Will".

"Did he go to a solicitor to make it?" Rosa enquired.

"No, he bought a form and did it himself."

"Let's hope he followed the instructions or it may be invalid."

Charlotte shrugged. "I don't expect it'll make much difference either way."

"Did he say why he was giving it to you for safekeeping?"

"I suppose I was the obvious person."

"And did he mention why he'd chosen that particular moment to make a will?"

"As I told you before, he envisaged the possibility of being attacked and even killed."

"You never said anything about a will when you came to see me last week," Rosa remarked suspiciously.

After considerable hesitation, Charlotte said, "The truth is that I've been in two minds what to do about it. As I was the only person who knew of its existence, I thought seriously about destroying it. After all, to find oneself the sole beneficiary of a murdered person's will could bring more aggro than it's worth." She gave Rosa a twisted sort of smile. "It isn't as if I'm going to become an overnight millionairess. I doubt whether Philip's assets total more than a few thousand and that could be an over-estimate."

Rosa gazed at her visitor trying to assess the truth of what she had just been told. On balance, she was inclined to believe Charlotte as there would seem to have been no point in concocting such a story.

She picked up the envelope and stared at it.

"You haven't tried to steam it open?" she asked with a small, quizzical smile.

"No," Charlotte said emphatically. "If I'd decided to destroy it, I didn't want to know the contents. I was on the very point of burning it this morning, but instead I've brought it round to you."

"It's a good thing you didn't destroy it. It would have been a serious criminal offence."

Charlotte shrugged. "Nobody would have known," she said.

Rosa picked up the ivory paper-knife from her desk. "Shall I open it?"

Charlotte gave a nod and Rosa slit open one end of the envelope and extracted the contents.

It was a printed will form of a sort that can be bought at most stationers. From a quick glance it appeared to have been properly completed. The testator's name and address and the date had all been completed.

In the space for the appointment of an executor, the name of Charlotte Bailey was written in. Then came the printed words

"I give and bequeath unto", followed in Atherly's own handwriting by "the aforesaid Charlotte Bailey everything I own and possess."

At the bottom of the page was Philip Atherly's signature and that of two witnesses.

"On the face of it, it's a valid will," Rosa remarked as she handed it to Charlotte who read it with studied care. "Who are Alice and Gordon Fenn, whose names appear as witnesses?"

"They run the small general store near to where he lived." She looked up and met Rosa's gaze. "What now?"

"One applies for probate, after which one distributes the assets and winds up the estate, none of which should take very long given the simple terms of the will. Incidentally, did he own his flat?"

"No, he took it over from a friend with the landlord's permission. It's fairly grotty and the area is due for redevelopment, so that he wouldn't have been able to stay there much longer, anyway. He didn't have any security of tenure." She paused. "Are you willing to do the necessary?"

If Rosa was to wash her hands of the

whole Atherly business, this was the right moment. Otherwise she would be committing herself not merely to winding up his estate, such as it was, but in effect to further investigating the mystery surrounding his death.

"All right," she said, after a brief internal struggle in which curiosity overcame the dictates of reason. At least she would now have some standing in the matter which she had previously lacked. "I can't do anything until I have a list of all his assets. Will you prepare one for me?"

Charlotte nodded. "That won't take long. Half a sheet of paper will be sufficient. One battered car, one TV set permanently on the blink and six pairs of socks, all with holes."

"You can lump all the clothing together and give it the sort of value it might fetch at a church bazaar. Did he own any pictures?"

"A couple of horrors painted by an ex-girl-friend who fancied herself as a female David Hockney."

"Any commercial value?"

"Five pounds for the two, provided the frames were thrown in."

Charlotte had clearly been right not to entertain any extravagant hopes as a beneficiary under Philip Atherly's will.

"What about his bank account?" Rosa asked suddenly.

"Overdrawn I should think."

Rosa frowned. "If so, the bank must have held some security."

"I've no idea."

"And there was the two thousand pounds he gave you to hold if I'd agree to look into his death, which he seems to have foreseen."

"He told me that was from the sale of his Mercedes," Charlotte said.

It was after she had gone that Rosa decided to phone Atherly's bank. She was put through to the assistant manager and explained her professional interest in their deceased client's account.

"Off the record, Miss Epton, I can tell you that Mr. Atherly's current account was about two thousand pounds overdrawn at the time of his death. I'm glad you've got in touch as I've been trying to find out who was acting for his estate. You understand, of course, that I'm telling you this in confidence in advance of your letting us have a copy of the grant of probate."

"I'm grateful for your help," Rosa said. "May I ask what security you held against his overdraft?"

The assistant manager gave a small, discreet cough. "It was a somewhat unusual form of security. A gold bar."

"Good gracious!" Rosa exclaimed. "How much is the bar worth?"

"At today's price around ten thousand pounds."

"Where on earth did he get it from?"

"That wouldn't be any of the bank's business, Miss Epton," the assistant manager said in a reproving tone.

After thanking him again for his help, Rosa rang off. The information she'd just been given had left her both stunned and thoughtful.

13

"**I**'VE obviously come back just in time," Peter Chen said, pulling Rosa into his side as they sat on the sofa in her flat.

He had arrived straight from the airport about two hours previously and, as usual on his return from a trip abroad, had only wanted to hear what she had been up to, brushing aside all enquiries about his own activities.

"It was just a routine trip," he said dismissively.

"You call a trip routine that takes you to Hong Kong, Singapore, Sydney and Melbourne?" Rosa said with a laugh. "The furthest I've been during your absence is Lewes prison."

"I want to hear about everything," he said. "About the girl you sat opposite in the train and the boy who was run over and killed and the murder. Everything."

And the surprising thing was, Rosa reflected, he actually meant it.

Assuming that he had eaten and drunk his way across the world, she hadn't immediately offered him food. But he had not been in the flat more than five minutes before he said, "I'm famished."

"Don't they feed you in first class any more?"

He made a face. "Airline food is as pretty as a colour plate and about as nourishing."

"You must have eaten something," Rosa said.

"I had some fish, which might have been chicken, covered in a tasteless gunge. Actually, the hot canapés are the best part of the meal."

"And drink? Presumably Scotch still tastes like Scotch?"

"They've not yet found a way of rendering that tasteless, thank goodness."

"So what do you want from the Air Epton galley?"

"Scrambled eggs. Yours are still the best in the world."

He accompanied her into the kitchen and, while she prepared his meal, Rosa gave him a blow-by-blow account of all that had happened during his absence.

When everything was ready she placed it on a tray which he carried into the living-room. Putting it down on the glass-topped coffee table in front of the sofa, he suddenly turned and wrapped his arms about her.

"This is the moment I've dreamt about all the time I've been away," he said, kissing her with lingering sensual desire.

"Your eggs will be getting cold," she said a trifle breathlessly when he eventually released her from his embrace.

"Is that all you were thinking?" he asked.

"No."

He grinned. "Thank goodness. I thought you might have gone off me."

Rosa knew that he didn't think anything of the sort, but let the remark pass.

"Why don't you open your present?" he asked.

"Present?" Rosa said lightly.

"Oh, good heavens alive. It's still in my overcoat pocket." He leapt up and dashed from the room, to return almost immediately with a small package wrapped in gold paper.

"Go on, open it," he said eagerly as he sat down and began to eat.

Rosa had never received opulent presents before she met Peter and always felt slightly embarrassed having to open them under his gaze. After all, their value in money terms was no guarantee she would like what he had bought her and, though so far she had never had to simulate her pleasure, the nervous strain told as she removed the outer wrapping.

"It's beautiful, Peter," she exclaimed as she peeled away the paper and opened the suede-covered box to reveal a platinum dress watch with an exquisite midnight-blue face. When she would ever have occasion to wear it was another matter.

"I thought you'd like it," he said with a touch of complacence. "I got it in Hong Kong."

"I thought at first it might be a small gold bar," Rosa said with a laugh and went on to tell him about Atherly's asset at the bank.

It was at this point Peter observed that he had obviously returned just in time.

"You evidently need a reliable sidekick,

Miss Epton. As to Atherly's gold bar, anyone can own one these days."

"Anyone with sufficient money to buy one," Rosa corrected him.

"I bet he didn't buy his. He must have acquired it."

"If it was stolen, presumably the bank would know. I didn't actually ask the assistant manager, but I got the impression there was nothing dodgy about Philip Atherly's gold bar; i.e. it has all the proper markings. So where do you think he obtained it?"

"He was either given it as a present or as payment for services rendered."

"Even you haven't got round to making presents of gold bars, Peter, so presumably it was payment for something he did."

"Something connected with drugs would be my guess."

"His girl-friend is sure he wasn't into drug dealing. He just smoked the occasional bit of cannabis."

"That sounds like what she chooses to believe," Peter said in a dismissive tone.

"He must have rendered someone a pretty substantial service to earn a £10,000 gold bar."

"Probably a final pay-off."

"I must get the bank to tell me more, like when he actually deposited it and what he said at the time."

"I don't expect he said anything except 'Please look after this for me'."

"Knowing Philip Atherly, it's doubtful if he would have said 'please'."

"I wonder if Mrs. Brigstock might be able to throw any light on the subject?"

"If Charlotte can't, I don't expect she can."

"She'd known him longer than Charlotte and he seems to have been a frequent visitor to Oakway in order to romp with her in the summer-house."

"True," Rosa observed thoughtfully. "I must say, she and her husband are the most obvious suspects. She certainly had opportunity and it's not difficult to pin a motive on her as well. The same goes for him, plus he had a more obvious motive. And yet the police still haven't made an arrest."

"They're probably awaiting the outcome of lab tests."

"If Atherly knew he was courting

danger, why did he push his luck beyond the limit?"

"And as you've said, what are you supposed to investigate?"

"There's only one logical answer to that, Peter. Namely, if he died, he wanted someone to look beyond the obvious facts in order to reach the truth."

"Why couldn't he have left a sealed letter or something of that sort saying in effect, 'If I'm found dead, this will be what happened . . .'?"

"It would have saved a lot of trouble if he had," Rosa remarked.

A few minutes later, Peter rested his head against Rosa's shoulder and quietly fell asleep. It seemed that jetlag had overtaken him before he even got home.

14

COLONEL FOX (christened Hugo but known as Reynard to his brother officers when he was a serving soldier) turned his head sharply to find his wife watching him from the doorway of his study.

"I thought you were upstairs," he said coldly.

"I've just come down. I heard movement in the study and came to see what you were doing." She glanced at his hand which was resting on the barrel of one of the guns. "Are you proposing to shoot this afternoon?"

He shook his head in a peremptory manner. "Have you been dusting in here?" he asked aggressively.

It was an unnecessary question as they both knew she had never dusted anything in her life. Others were employed to keep the house clean.

"No. Why do you ask?"

"Because someone's had the gun cupboard open."

"But you always keep it locked."

"I know that," he observed tartly, "but the key's not hard to find. Several people know where I keep it."

"You're probably imagining things."

He drew his mouth into a forbidding line beneath his moustache.

"Somebody," he said slowly and with heavy emphasis, "has definitely opened the cupboard."

"How can you be sure?"

"I know."

"Perhaps it was Joanna when she was here at the weekend."

"Why should she have wanted to open it?"

"Why should anyone, except yourself?" his wife enquired in a quietly maddening tone.

It wasn't a question he was disposed to try to answer. He was still angry that she had taken him by surprise. Normally she never came downstairs until the gong was sounded for lunch.

"Are we having lunch early today?" he

asked testily. "If so, I think somebody might have told me."

"I'm sure it'll be on the table at the usual time. Mrs. Ollerton's always punctual."

Mrs. Ollerton, the wife of one of his farm-workers, came in every day to cook lunch and wash up. Two other women shared the cleaning duties, coming in on alternate days, and yet a fourth was employed to prepare their evening meal.

He gave his wife a look of barely concealed irritation. "Why don't you go and sit down? You're standing in a draught and you know how easily you catch cold." He turned away so that he failed to observe her own fleeting expression of amused contempt. She turned and moved away without saying anything further.

He wondered how long she had been standing there watching him before he became aware of her presence. Not that it really mattered, save that, like most people, he disliked being taken by surprise. What gave him greater food for thought was that somebody had been showing an interest in his gun cupboard.

If it was Joanna, it could only mean that she believed he might have murdered Atherly and wanted to see if there was any evidence.

He smiled grimly at the thought. As if he would have been that careless! It was, however, a further reminder that his daughter bore out the old saying about still waters running deep. It was never easy to know what was going on in her mind. He knew that her experience with Atherly had left her badly scarred, though it never occurred to him that his own conduct in the affair had aggravated matters. He had always been a strict but undemonstrative father and had never been afflicted by any form of self-doubt in his handling of Joanna's traumatic ordeal.

He would have dearly liked to have a son who would have reflected his own red-bloodedness. Instead, he had a wife who was little more than a pallid cut-out (small wonder that his sexual needs had had to be appeased elsewhere), and a daughter who was little better.

Fortunately, perhaps, he had never sought an emotional relationship with another woman. Fortunate, because it would have been bound to lead to complications. As it was, his sexual appetites could be assuaged more simply. Even so, he had had occasion to wonder whether his involvement with Sally Brigstock was entirely wise. Admittedly she was a damned attractive girl who was married to a sexless pedagogue and who had given him a come-hither look the very first time they met at a cocktail party in the neighbourhood.

Nevertheless, he had trodden warily and it was some time before he took up her unspoken challenge to join her in bed. The first time that happened was during the school holidays when her husband was away in Cambridge on a seminar. Since then, the experience had been repeated only twice, the last occasion, as he now recalled with some mortification, having taken place in the old summer-house.

He had had no idea that she was all the while carrying on with Philip Atherly. She'd kept that bit of information to herself. It was his belief that Atherly had left the district for good and disappeared into the distant blue. It had come as a disagreeable shock to learn otherwise. In his view Sally Brigstock had been both irresponsible and downright deceitful. And yet he was not as angry as he might have been and when later she had sought his advice, he had done more than offer her mere words.

And now Atherly had met a fate he richly deserved and the police were floundering in their search for his murderer, while he, Hugo Fox, could observe events coolly from a distance.

Everything had worked out better than might have been expected, except that he would still like to know who had been meddling with his gun cupboard. And why.

15

DETECTIVE CHIEF INSPECTOR YULE gave the young woman sitting opposite him an appraising gaze which she met without a flicker of concern.

He was wondering if she had really provided him with the breakthrough he had been looking for. If so, it was in an entirely unexpected direction.

He knew from her original statement that she was thirty-two years old, unmarried and that she had only arrived at Easter House School as matron that term.

"And you're saying that Mrs. Brigstock admitted to you she had committed the murder?" he said in a speculative voice.

"Yes."

"And yet you never mentioned it when I first interviewed you?"

"Because I wished to consider my position very carefully before coming forward."

"That means you might have been ready to conceal a vital piece of information."

She gave a shrug. "I didn't want to rush into anything."

"And what decided you to come to the police at this late hour?"

"I felt my obligation to do so outweighed other considerations. Once I'd made up my mind, I handed in my notice and said I'd be leaving at the end of the term."

"Did you say why?"

"I merely said that I had been completely unsettled by all that had happened and that I didn't feel able to stay."

"When Mrs. Brigstock made this admission of murder to you, did you believe her?"

Judy Kent was pensive for a while. "I really don't know whether I did or I didn't. I'd met her for the first time at the beginning of term and I had no personal yardstick by which to judge her." She paused and bit her lip. "She certainly wasn't somebody whose word I'd regard as gospel truth. From all I'd heard about her, she could be a bit mercurial in her behaviour."

"Unstable, you mean?"

"Let's say unpredictable." She smiled wryly. "Save where men were concerned. There, I gathered, she was wholly predictable."

"Just tell me again the precise circumstances in which she made this admission to you."

Yule hoped that by getting her to repeat her story, he could test its veracity. Any substantial deviation from what she had previously said would tell against her truthfulness. Despite all the years he had spent seeing the darker side of human nature, he still maintained a reasonable faith in people's sense of decency and responsibility. But nobody could pretend that Judy Kent had shown a sense of responsibility in withholding such vital information in a murder enquiry. He viewed her excuse with scepticism. If the case should turn on her evidence, she could expect to be savagely attacked by the defence. He wondered if she was aware of this. Meanwhile she was reliving the events of that grisly night.

"When I first saw Mrs. Brigstock, it was shortly after her return from discovering the body. Mr. Winslow asked me to stay with her while he and Fred went to investigate. She was in her husband's study and seemed utterly distraught. Mr. Winslow had given her some brandy and this helped her a bit to get her emotions under control."

"Was she saying anything in particular?"

"She just kept on repeating, 'It was horrible, his face was a mass of red pulp.'"

"Were those her exact words?"

Judy frowned. "Yes, I'm sure they were."

"Please go on."

"I suggested she should go up to her bedroom and I'd send for the doctor. She was obviously in a state of shock. But she said she wanted to stay downstairs until Mr. Winslow and Fred returned. . . ."

"Did she mention her husband during this time?"

"No, not at all."

Yule gave her a nod to continue.

"Eventually she agreed to go up to her

room and I went off to fetch her a cup of hot, sweet tea. She was wandering about the bedroom in an aimless sort of way when I got there. She drank the tea and seemed by then to have got her emotions more or less under control. She was obviously still deeply shocked by her experience, but she was no longer hysterical. From time to time she stared at the bed and gave a little shiver as though it were the last place she wanted to find herself." She made a face. "Quite frankly, from all I'd heard since I arrived at the school, I was surprised that Mr. and Mrs. Brigstock still shared the same bed.

"While she was drinking the tea, I went across to the window to see if there was any sign of Mr. Winslow and Fred returning across the fields. I knew they'd taken a flashlight. While I was peering out, I had a funny sort of feeling that Mrs. Brigstock was staring hard at my back. I turned round to see that she had a very strange look on her face. Before I could speak, she said, without any sort of warning, 'Have you ever wanted to murder anyone, Judy?'"

Woman Police Constable Whitaker, who

was present, leaned quietly forward like a cat preparing to stalk its prey.

"I wasn't sure if she was being serious," Judy went on, "though it did strike me as a very odd thing to say in the circumstances, so I replied to the effect I could cheerfully have murdered one or two of the more troublesome boys. She ignored that and said, 'Some murders are justified, you know.' Then before I could think what to say, she went on, 'You probably don't think I look capable of murder, but I am.' 'What on earth are you trying to tell me?' I asked and she said, 'Isn't it obvious?' and sort of smirked. Fortunately the doctor arrived shortly after that and gave her a sedative which put her out like a light." She gave Yule an ironical look. "Perhaps you'd like to give me a truth drug and have me repeat it all over again."

There had certainly been no serious discrepancies in the two accounts she had provided and he felt he had no reason to disbelieve her. It was too strange a story to have been made up out of malice. If, for some perverted reason, she had wanted to frame Sally Brigstock, she could have done it more easily. The question that now

172

occupied Yule's mind was whether it did actually amount to a confession of murder. That was the inference, but even so could it be regarded as reliable? Might Sally Brigstock not have been in such a state of shock that her imagination had free-wheeled into the realm of fantasy?

"Looking back now, Miss Kent," he said, "do you believe she was trying to tell you she had just committed a murder?"

She gave a small, helpless shrug. "I've no idea. Obviously I've thought about it a lot, but I've still no idea. Also you have to remember that when she said it, I didn't actually know there'd been a murder. Mr. Winslow had merely said something about a bad accident. . . ."

Yule nodded. He had also taken note of this. Whatever Peter Winslow had said, it was clear that Sally Brigstock knew it was murder. Winslow would have to be seen again and have his recollection checked.

Meanwhile, it was apparent that the headmaster's wife must be re-interviewed and questioned about her supposed confession. And that as a matter of urgency.

Detective Inspector Hart paced up and

down while Yule sat staring out of the window. The scene was once more Yule's office where they awaited Sally Brigstock's arrival.

When Yule had phoned the school he had been told she was out and it was believed that the police station was her intended port of call.

That could only mean that she had got wind of Judy Kent's visit and wished to put her own version of events on record.

"That's bloody suspicious in itself," Hart observed. "She knows the Kent woman can sink her."

"It's still unusual for a murder suspect to come knocking at the door of the lion's den," Yule remarked.

"Not in my experience it isn't," Hart said in a scoffing tone. "It's no more than a daring move in a dangerous game. You mark my words, we've got her on a hook and we mustn't let her wriggle free."

Though he had said "we", Yule was aware that he meant "you".

"If she did murder Atherly, where'd she get the gun? After all, we know it couldn't have been her husband's. The lab found a spider living in the barrel of his."

DI Hart's expression registered contempt for such a niggling point.

"One of the other masters may own one. As I've said before, shotguns in the country are two a penny. Anyway, the boys used to shoot on that range behind the school."

"With a .22 rifle, not a shotgun," Yule pointed out. "But even if Mrs. Brigstock did somehow get hold of a gun, what did she do with it afterwards? She didn't have it with her when she arrived back and was greeted by Winslow at the side entrance."

"She could have hidden it somewhere and retrieved it later. No problem about that. Or she may have had an accomplice."

Yule remained silent. He was used to his DI firing off theories like a proverbial wild man of the west. He did, however, wish that Hart hadn't returned to the station at the moment he had. He would much prefer to interview Mrs. Brigstock on his own. But to try to exclude the DI would be an invitation to trouble.

His phone buzzed and he lifted the receiver.

"OK, bring them up," he said with a frown.

"Them?" Hart said sharply. "Don't say she's brought her husband, too?"

"No. A solicitor."

The door opened and WPC Whitaker stood aside to let the visitors enter.

Sally Brigstock was wearing a thick, canary yellow sweater and a pair of well-cut jeans. If she felt under threat of arrest, she certainly showed no sign of it.

Behind her came a young man, dressed in a dark suit. He wore a pair of gold-rimmed spectacles and his face showed vestigial signs of acne.

"I'm Barry Hayler from Draycott and Wentworth," he said solemnly. "I'm here to represent Mrs. Brigstock."

Yule had heard that the firm had recently taken on a newly qualified solicitor, but he hadn't expected to see someone who looked quite so wet behind the ears. For his part, DI Hart was eyeing the solicitor as though he were something unpleasant deposited on his doorstep.

When everyone was seated, Yule opened proceedings.

"It so happens, Mrs. Brigstock, that I was wanting to see you, but when I phoned the school, I was told you were already on your way here. Quite a coincidence."

"Let's cut the small talk!" Hayler said in a tone that made Yule blink. Though he might look youthfully gormless, he was plainly intent on serving notice that first impressions could be deceptive.

"Very well," Yule replied equably. "What is it you want to see me about?"

Hayler frowned. "I think it would be better in the circumstances if you stated your business first."

Ignoring DI Hart's expression of impending apoplexy, Yule turned towards Sally Brigstock. Though she looked perfectly calm, he noticed that she was quietly shredding the tissue she was holding.

"Cast your mind back to the night of the murder after you'd returned to the house," he said. "I understand you talked about what had happened to the matron, Judy Kent."

"I may have spoken to her, but I don't remember what I said. I was in a state of shock at the time."

"According to her, you said something

that could be interpreted as an admission of murder."

"Hold it there," Hayler broke in. "Surely you should caution my client before you make accusations of that sort. And if you do caution her, I shall advise her to exercise her right of remaining silent."

Yule gave the young solicitor a thoughtful look. He might know the ground rules, but that didn't make him a smart lawyer.

"All right. Then you'd better tell me what's brought *you* here today. Brought you of your own free will, I might add."

Sally Brigstock shot her solicitor the sort of look a player might give her tennis partner who has just served a double fault at a crucial stage of the match.

Hayler swallowed and leaned forward with an earnest expression.

"Mrs. Brigstock thought it right to let you know that Miss Kent is under notice to leave at the end of the present term. Her appointment hasn't proved satisfactory and she has been told to go."

"Who took that decision?"

"My client, in consultation with the headmaster."

"And why should this unremarkable event necessitate Mrs. Brigstock visiting the police station with her lawyer?"

Hayler assumed a portentous expression of the sort that's part of a lawyer's stock-in-trade.

"Unfortunately, Miss Kent has seen fit to spread malicious rumours about my client among the staff."

"Such as?"

"That my client knows more about the murder than she has told the police."

"I presume you knew that Miss Kent came to the station earlier today?"

"Not exactly knew," Hayler replied with a slight squirm.

"But you were aware of her intention to come?"

"I don't see that any of this is relevant," the solicitor said tersely.

"Like hell it's relevant," Hart broke in. "It's my guess that the only purpose of your visit is to try and spike Judy Kent's guns."

Yule let out a quiet sigh. It was like

having an obstreperous dog in the room. Aloud he said:

"I agree with Inspector Hart. It's obviously relevant. I'll repeat my question. Were you aware of Miss Kent's intention to come to the police?"

"My client had heard something to that effect."

"And so you hoped to get in first?"

"I resent the inference in that remark," Hayler said huffily.

"According to Miss Kent, there was no question of her being dismissed. It was she who gave in her notice."

"She's just lying again," Sally Brigstock said. "She's out to make mischief."

"If you're right, it's something a good deal worse than mischief," Yule observed. "What she's done amounts to a crime."

"Then I hope you'll take the appropriate action," Hayler said severely.

"That'll depend on who we believe." He focused his attention back on Mrs. Brigstock. "Do you recall saying anything to Miss Kent that could have been construed as a confession of murder?"

"Certainly not."

"You had a motive for murdering Philip Atherly, did you not?"

"Who says I did?"

"I'm asking you."

"I advise my client not to answer that question," Hayler broke in. "Anyway, you've still not cautioned her."

It's like being caught on a carousel, Yule reflected. The same bit of scenery keeps coming round. Before he could say anything, the solicitor continued:

"If Miss Kent has been inventing stories about my client, as is apparently the case, you'd do well to ask yourself why she has waited this long to bring her damaging information to the police. Why didn't she come forward immediately?"

His tone was hectoring and, though he might be young and inexperienced, he was sharp enough to direct his counter-attack at the weaker aspects of the case against his client.

Yule was in no mood to become involved in argument, nor did he see any advantage to be gained in prolonging the interview, whatever DI Hart might be thinking. He now believed that the matron had told him the truth. What was more pertinent, however, was whether Sally Brigstock's confession of murder was genuine.

And there still remained the mystery of how she had got hold of a gun and what had happened to it afterwards. Until he had an answer to that, there could be no question of preferring a charge.

For the moment the evidence against both Mr. *and* Mrs. Brigstock remained inconclusive.

If Judy Kent's information was a breakthrough of sorts, it seemed merely to lift him out of one stockade and drop him in another.

16

IT was with relief that Rosa greeted her partner's return to the office in the middle of that week. She thought he still looked frail, but he proclaimed himself fit enough to face the office.

"Susan began suggesting jobs that needed doing about the house," he said, "so I knew it was time to come back. Tell me what's been happening while I've been away."

Rosa told him, finishing up with an account of her Saturday visit to Oakway.

"All sounds a bit incestuous," he remarked.

"Incest is about the only thing that's missing."

"I used the word in a descriptive sense. Everyone is tangled with everyone else and there's a strong reek of sexual motivation."

"So you think Atherly's death had a sexual motive?"

Robin smiled. "It's a reasonable guess. Most murders do. What's your theory?"

Rosa let out a loud sigh. "I wish I had one. I keep on changing my mind. What sticks with me is that Philip Atherly had a premonition about his death and didn't want anyone taken in by the obvious. Hence this strange wish that I should look into it, should it happen."

"You say 'taken in by the obvious'. What is the obvious in this context?"

"That the headmaster of Easter House School murdered him from motives of revenge or jealousy. Or that Mrs. Brigstock killed him because he wanted to end their relationship—if in fact he did."

"Age-old motives in both cases."

"Perhaps I ought to be looking for a spanking new motive."

"There are only the old ones. Jealousy, revenge, greed and protection of one's security. And I wouldn't think that Atherly's murder falls within the last category. They're the people who kill to avoid detection."

Rosa was thoughtful. "I wonder. . . ? I wonder. . . ?"

"What?"

"Whether he mayn't have been murdered to ensure his silence."

"Could be, I suppose. That gold bar in his bank gives his lifestyle an interesting dimension."

"I don't see how it could have provided a motive for his murder."

"Agreed, but it indicates that he was probably caught up in some activity outside the law. Not even our most colourful clients have ever tried to pay us in gold bars. Perhaps we ought to raise our charges and refuse to accept cheques."

He produced a tin of throat lozenges and proffered it to Rosa.

"Are they any good?" she enquired.

"They're nasty enough, so they must be." He paused. "Incidentally, what about the girl on the train, any further news of her?"

Rosa shook her head. "I haven't liked to bother Inspector Gainham again."

"Why don't you drive up and visit her mother? Northampton, isn't it?" he asked in an apparently casual tone.

Rosa stared at him in surprise. "What on earth for?"

"To satisfy your curiosity, that's what for. Now that I'm back, take a day off. I'm sure Mrs. Forbes would be more than pleased to meet one of the last people who saw her daughter. And I'm sure Peter Chen would be delighted to accompany you," he added slyly.

A slow smile spread across Rosa's face. "I do believe you've made my day," she said in a voice that conveyed both pleasure and a trace of excitement. "As a matter of fact, it was a thought that had crossed my mind, but I was hoping somebody else would suggest it."

Peter Chen arrived outside Rosa's flat just before nine o'clock the next morning. Twenty minutes later they had reached the M1 and his BMW reacted like an eager greyhound let off its leash. Though she always said that nothing would persuade her to swap her small Honda for a larger car, the fact was she was never happier than being driven by Peter. He was a skilled driver and made it seem effortless.

Motorways (the M1 in particular) invariably reminded Rosa of a headlong dash to perdition. There was something horrendous about the unceasing flow of pounding lorries. She wondered whether it was still the same on Christmas Day, but

186

had no wish to find out. Not even the soothing, velvety tones of Nat King Cole could dispel the feeling of waiting doom. It was a relief when they turned off and were soon afterwards entering the outskirts of Northampton.

In Rosa's experience, building societies tended to huddle together, as though each was unwilling to let its competitors out of sight.

"Let's park here," she said, when they found themselves in what was plainly the right area. "We can ask where the South Midlands Building Society is."

"We'll spot it if we drive round a bit," he said with his customary obstinacy when it came to parking the car. A moment later he exclaimed, "I saw it then. Up that street to the left."

"We can't turn left, it's a one-way system," Rosa replied with exaggerated patience. "Look, there's a public car park two hundred yards ahead."

In the event, he found a meter space in a side street and they got out before Nat King Cole could give a third rendering of "A Nightingale Sang in Berkeley Square".

The offices of the South Midlands

Building Society looked and smelt new and exuded a scented warmth not normally associated with the feverish flutterings of interest rates.

Rosa approached a desk which had a sign marked "Reception" on its forward edge.

"Is it possible to speak to Mrs. Forbes?" she asked.

The girl behind the desk, who had switched on a waxy smile as they reached her, now turned it down to half-power.

"Which Mrs. Forbes?" she said. "Mrs. Eileen Forbes or Mrs. Patricia Forbes?"

"Mrs. Patricia Forbes."

"And your name?"

"Rosa Epton. Mrs. Forbes doesn't know me, but I'm a solicitor from London."

"If you care to take a seat over there," she said, indicating a long wall sofa a safe distance from her desk, "I'll find out if Mrs. Forbes is free."

"I thought for a moment she was going to push the alarm button," Peter remarked as they sat down. "She looked at us as if we were an updated, multiracial version of Bonnie and Clyde."

About three minutes later, a door

beyond the reception desk opened and a woman came through. She had a homely figure and a head of unnatural blonde curls.

As she came towards them, Rosa and Peter got up.

"Mrs. Forbes? My name's Rosa Epton and this is a friend of mine, Peter Chen."

"I seem to know your name, but I'm afraid I can't place it," Mrs. Forbes said vaguely.

"I sat opposite your daughter on a train shortly before she disappeared."

"Yes, of course. Now I remember." She looked suddenly hopeful. "Do you have news of Trina?"

"I'm afraid not."

"Oh! I hoped . . ." The sentence tailed off with a forlorn shrug.

"I'd very much like to have a talk with you, Mrs. Forbes. Could we meet somewhere?"

"I usually take an early lunch. If you like, I could meet you at the Cedar Tree at twelve. It's a café fifty yards down the street on the right hand side."

"Splendid. We'll get there first and grab a table."

"What exactly do you want to talk about?" she asked with a sudden frown as she turned to go.

Rosa took a deep breath. "I have no evidence to prove it, but I can't help wondering whether your daughter's disappearance mayn't be connected in some way with another event that took place in Sussex about the same time."

Mrs. Forbes gave her head a puzzled shake. "I'll talk to anyone who can help me find Trina," she said after a pause.

As they walked away from the building society office, Peter said, "You never told me you believed Trina's disappearance might be connected with the murder."

"She caught me on the hop. I had to say something, otherwise I felt she might have second thoughts about meeting us."

"Does that mean you don't really believe there's any connection?"

Rosa slipped her hand into his. "I don't really know. Ask me again after we've talked to Mrs. Forbes."

The Cedar Tree was one of those chintzy establishments where ladies in flowered smocks served nourishing, home-made food in portions suitable for anyone on a diet.

"I usually come here," Mrs. Forbes said when she joined them. "It's convenient and I only want something light as I cook an evening meal when I get home."

She looked about her awkwardly as if embarrassed at being seen in strange company.

"It's fine for us," Rosa said, hoping to put her at her ease. "Incidentally, my friend is also a solicitor. You must be wondering why we've come. The truth is that your daughter's face has haunted me ever since I sat opposite her in that train, so that when I read about her disappearance, I immediately got in touch with the police. But as time has gone by I felt I must meet you, even though I have no tidings to bear, good or bad." She paused. "The last I heard was when I spoke to Inspector Gainham and he told me you had received a phone call from Trina who was obviously somewhere abroad. Has there been any further news?"

"She's phoned once more since then. She just said she was all right and I wasn't to worry. But what mother wouldn't worry?" she exclaimed bitterly.

"She didn't give you any clue as to where she was?"

Mrs. Forbes shook her head. "It was a very bad line with a lot of atmospherics and I could hardly hear what she was saying. Naturally, I asked her where she was and why she didn't come home. She said something about not being able to yet, but that she was all right." She gave Rosa an intent look. "The police informed me, of course, of what you'd told them, but I should like to hear it from your own lips."

"Of course . . ."

When Rosa had finished describing the fateful train journey, Mrs. Forbes said in a wistful tone, "Wherever Trina went, her Sony Walkman went too. I used to tell her that one day the world would blow up and she'd be found still plugged into the thing."

"What used she to listen to for the most part?"

"Pop music. Endless pop music. In that way, she was no different from most girls of her age. They go through these phases."

"Didn't we all," Rosa said with a smile.

"I used to try my father's patience playing Elvis records non-stop."

"I still quite like some of his music."

"My father was a country parson to whom Kathleen Ferrier was the only singer worthy of the name and Bach the only composer." She paused for a moment. "Obviously Trina wasn't listening to pop music when she tore off the headset. So what?"

"Nobody seems to have any idea, least of all the police."

"It must have been something that badly scared her. I suppose it could have been some form of threat."

"Who on earth would want to threaten Trina? She wasn't mixed up with bad people."

Rosa gave her a helpless look. These were the words of a loving and emotionally involved mother, not of a coldly reasoning person.

"I wonder what she was doing in Sussex that day?"

"She'd never mentioned any friends living in that area."

"And yet the odds are that she had visited somebody there. What about boyfriends? An attractive girl like her must have had admirers."

"There was a boy here she used to go with before she moved to London. Gary Boyce was his name. But they split up after nearly a year together and he has since married a local girl. She was always mentioning different names, but I don't think there was anyone regular. We never met any of them and whenever I enquired after one it was usually to find that he had been replaced in her affections."

"Did she ever mention anyone called Philip?" Rosa asked suddenly.

"Not that I recall. As I say, we never met any of her London friends, so one tended not to remember their names, particularly as there was such a brisk turnover." After a reflective pause she went on, "You said earlier that you believed Trina's disappearance might be connected with something else that had happened. What were you referring to?"

Rosa drew a deep breath aware that both Peter and Trina's mother were watching her intently.

"On the day I sat opposite Trina in the train, I read in a local paper about a schoolboy who had been knocked down and killed by a hit-and-run driver who had never been traced. There was a mystery about what the boy was doing out of his dormitory when it happened. It's a mystery that remains unsolved. Then some time later a man was murdered in the grounds of the school the boy attended. The dead man was someone named Philip Atherly who had been a client of mine. His murder also remains unsolved, though not through any lack of suspects. . . ."

"I'm sure Trina had nothing whatsoever to do with what you've just described," Mrs. Forbes said with a touch of anger.

"I agree it's pure speculation on my part," Rosa said with a sigh. "Probably because two of the events impinged upon my consciousness on the same day. The newspaper article about the boy's death and sitting opposite your daughter in the train."

"That doesn't relate them together."

"I know, and yet I have this feeling that they may be connected." She paused before going on. "Supposing Trina knew something about the boy's death and is being kept out of the way so that she can't go to the police with her information."

"Isn't that rather far-fetched?" Mrs. Forbes enquired brusquely. "There's no indication that Trina's being kept out of the way, as you put it. If that were so, she wouldn't have been able to phone me."

"Did it sound as if she were repeating what she'd been told to say?"

Mrs. Forbes ground out her cigarette.

"If you must know," she said bitterly, "it sounded as if she had a guilty conscience about worrying me and her father, but wasn't prepared to do anything about it, other than tell us not to worry." She glanced at her watch. "I must be getting back to the office. I'm glad to have met you, Miss Epton." She stood up and held out her hand to say goodbye. "This may sound funny, but if Trina were dead, I'd know where I was. As it is, the suspense of not knowing what's happened to her and, even more, why she's behaving like this has completely destroyed any peace of mind I ever had."

"I'm sure she's not being deliberately heartless," Rosa said. "It's just that young people can be thoughtless because too often they see things only through their own eyes. The fact that she's phoned you shows that she is aware of the anxiety she's caused you."

"Whatever the outcome, things can never be the same between us."

With this bleak observation still hanging in the air, Mrs. Forbes turned and left the café. Rosa gave Peter a helpless look.

"You've kept very quiet," she said.

"I had nothing to contribute," he said primly.

"You obviously think I made a mess of things."

"I think you may have increased her worries by suggesting that her daughter was mixed up in criminal activities."

Rosa looked at him in distress.

"Perhaps it was a silly idea to come, but I thought that meeting Trina's mother might help to exorcise the memory that haunts me."

"I know," he said quietly. "But do you really believe there's a connection between Trina's disappearance and the other events?"

Rosa was silent for a while.

"They're inextricably woven together in my mind," she said at last.

"There isn't a shred of evidence to connect them."

"Intuition tells me they are."

"I admit it's the best intuition I've ever come across, but it's still not infallible."

As they drove back to London, Rosa reflected that girls of Trina's age who suddenly start behaving unpredictably and out of character often do so because they are under the powerful influence of love. Though it certainly couldn't have been any message of love that caused her to tear off her headset in the train and look so scared.

She felt dispirited by the thought that she might have added to Mrs. Forbes's anxiety and knew that somehow she must make amends.

17

HEAVY mist hung over the countryside when Rosa and Peter drove down to Oakway two days later. There was the sort of dank stillness associated with a Victorian cemetery.

They arrived at the Pheasant public house to find the car park almost deserted. Peter parked beneath an ancient oak tree that stood in one corner, but regretted doing so when it dripped on to his head as he got out. He glared at it and stepped quickly out of harm's way.

"So this is Oakway," he said as Rosa came round the back of the car to join him. "No wonder boys run away from school in a place like this."

"Jason Cutler wasn't running away," she said firmly.

He put an arm round her shoulder and propelled her towards the pub entrance.

"I could do with a very large whisky, but I suppose I mustn't as I'm driving."

"Also it's early in the day."

"And we haven't come to a pub in order to drink," he intoned.

"Exactly."

Jim Thesiger looked up from the racing page of the paper he was reading when they entered. He gave Rosa a small, quizzical smile.

"So what brings you back?"

Ignoring the question, she said, "I've brought a friend with me."

The landlord eyed Peter with obvious curiosity. "Wouldn't happen to know what's going to win the two thirty at Lingfield this afternoon, would you?" he enquired in a supercilious tone.

"Blair's Delight," Peter said promptly. "It's joint favourite."

Jim Thesiger stared at him in astonishment. "So you're a racing man?"

"I have the occasional gamble. But what I need at the moment is a drink."

"Of course. What's it to be?"

"A glass of ginger wine for Miss Epton and half a pint of lager for me."

Rosa had listened to their exchange with secret amusement. She knew there were times when Peter enjoyed exercising a degree of quiet authority and that it was usually people like Jim Thesiger who produced them. The thought of ginger wine hadn't entered her mind, but she now realised it was the perfect drink for the day.

"Still interested in Oakway's crimes?" Jim Thesiger said as he put their drinks on the counter.

"Have there been any further developments?" Rosa asked.

"The police have had Mrs. Brigstock in for more questioning, but didn't hold her. If you ask me they ought to charge both of them, the headmaster and his wife, and let them fight it out in court."

"You really believe one of them killed Atherly?"

"Yes, I do." He paused. "Life must be bloody impossible at the school, so it would be a merciful way of closing the place down. I wouldn't expect any boys to return after the Christmas holidays, so it might just as well fold now."

"Did the police have some fresh evidence against Mrs. Brigstock?"

"Rumour has it that the matron opened her mouth and told the police how Mrs.

Brigstock had confessed to her that she'd committed the murder."

"But presumably the police didn't feel sufficiently sure of their ground to prefer a charge?"

"One of their motorcycle patrol officers lives in the next village and drops by here from time to time. He says the officer in charge of the investigation, Chief Inspector Yule, is one of those belt and braces merchants. Never makes a move until he's a hundred per cent certain." He paused and gave a resigned shrug. "For all I know, I could be on his list of suspects. After all, I've never hidden my feelings about Atherly. I could cheerfully have broken his neck when he cleared off owing me money."

"That's somewhat different from viciously murdering him several years later."

"It's still no more than he deserved. And I don't mind if you quote me on that."

"Does Colonel Fox share that view?"

The landlord frowned. "The Colonel doesn't discuss his views with the likes of me," he replied tartly.

Rosa decided not to remind him how he and the Colonel had spent considerable time deep in conversation during her previous visit. Her recollection was of two conspirators at work. They certainly hadn't been discussing the weather. Of that she was quite sure.

A customer came in and Jim Thesiger moved away to serve him. Having done so, however, he showed no sign of returning to the end of the bar where Rosa and Peter were standing.

"Shall we eat here?" Rosa said.

"Might as well. Then leave. We're not going to get any more out of *him*," Peter observed, nodding in the direction of the landlord. "He obviously didn't like your question about the Colonel and has closed ranks against us. I expect he'd like to know what specifically has brought you back here, but let him wonder. He put in his pennyworth of poison against the Brigstocks and that's that."

It was at this moment that Gina Thesiger appeared from behind the scenes.

"Oh, hello," she said in a sunny voice, "come back for more of our cornbeef hash, have you? If so, I'm afraid you'll be disappointed as it's not on today. But I can thoroughly recommend the sweet and sour chicken served with rice." She gave Peter a mischievous smile. "Just like your mother makes," she added with a gust of laughter.

"Meanwhile your crimes remain unsolved, I gather," Rosa remarked.

"I hope mine always will, dear," she said, "but I know what you mean." Her expression clouded over. "The whole village is seething with rumour and everyone is whispering behind everyone else's back. It's not a bit nice."

"What's the latest rumour?" Rosa asked hopefully.

Gina glanced nervously towards her husband who was serving a group of men who'd just come in.

"That the dead man had been seeing Colonel Fox's daughter up in London and that the Colonel found out—"

"Here, come and give me a hand," her husband's voice cut in.

"I'm just fetching in the food," she called back.

"It can wait. I need a hand. Now."

"I'd better go and help him out or—"

"Gina!" he shouted angrily.

"Just coming, love." And she hurried away.

"He'll probably thump her for talking to strangers," Peter observed.

"I wonder if it's true that Philip Atherly had taken up with Colonel Fox's daughter again?" Rosa said in a thoughtful tone.

"It shouldn't be too difficult to find out. Leave it to me to discover her address in town."

"I suppose Charlotte may know, but I doubt it."

"No harm in asking her."

"If it's true that he was, it strengthens the Colonel's motive for murder."

"Tenfold," Peter remarked. He gazed along the bar to where the landlord and his wife were getting drinks for a further influx of customers. "Let's go and eat elsewhere. I feel we've outstayed our welcome. And if the sweet and sour chicken really is like anything my mother made, it'll be uneatable."

After a lunch of freshly baked crusty bread, farm butter and a hunk of well matured cheddar cheese in the pub of a neighbouring village, they returned to the car and headed for the school.

"No point in coming all this way and not calling there," Peter had remarked and Rosa agreed. "We can pretend to be prospective parents," he added. "That'll give them something to think about."

As they drove up an avenue of quietly dripping trees towards the house, shrill cries and yelps, mingled with blasts on a whistle, reached their ears. Small figures could be seen dashing about wildly in the mist.

"Play up, Easter House," an adult voice shouted in exhortation.

The football pitch was to their right and Peter pulled up on the opposite grass verge. There were blobs of people round the perimeter of the field and a scattering of boys, some of whom were relieving their boredom by chasing and wrestling with one another. The half dozen or so adults stamped their feet in an endeavour to keep warm and gave vent to periodic sharp barks of encouragement.

"Small wonder the British usually win their wars," Peter murmured as he got out of the car.

"But they're enjoying it," Rosa remarked.

"I know. And don't say it's character-forming because I know that, too. Murder, sudden death, adultery and heaven knows what else besides can go on under their little noses and they still charge around chasing a football in a thick mist."

"Good afternoon," a voice behind them suddenly said. "Are you with the opposition?"

"Opposition?" Rosa said in a puzzled tone as she turned round.

"St. Oswald's. I assumed you weren't Easter House supporters." Then before Rosa could reply, the woman went on, "I can't think why anyone should want to watch football on a day like this. Incidentally, I'm Sally Brigstock. My husband's the headmaster of Easter House." She pointed at the only adult on the field of play. "That's him. He's refereeing the match, in case you wondered what he's doing out there."

"My name's Rosa Epton," Rosa said quickly. "And this is a friend of mine, Peter Chen."

"Rosa Epton, did you say? Then you

must be the person who defended Philip Atherly on a drugs charge."

"Yes."

"Have you come here specifically to see me?"

"That was certainly my hope," Rosa said, seizing her opportunity.

"We'll go up to the house. We can't possibly talk here," she said, glancing about her with disdain. "Come on, let's disappear into the mist."

"Is Mr. Chen your partner?" she asked as they walked away.

"No. Peter's in practice on his own. Our two practices are as different as fillet steak from meat loaf. His is the steak."

As the whistle blasts and shouts receded behind them, Sally Brigstock said, "As you can probably guess, life here isn't very easy at the moment."

"I realise what a nightmare the school must have been through."

"The school? What about me?"

"You and everyone else," Rosa said in a mollifying tone.

"We have to try and keep up pretences, but it becomes more difficult every day. A lot of our parents live abroad, so are blithely unaware of all the traumas. They have to rely on their sons' letters for school news and we simply censor the more lurid accounts. Actually, my husband has written to all the parents telling them not to believe all they hear as everything is under control and school life goes on despite what he refers to as 'certain unfortunate events'." She pulled a face. "You might think that the understatement of the century with both the headmaster and his wife suspected of murder." She suddenly looked across at a high brick wall with a wooden door set in it. "That's the boys' garden," she said. "Jason Cutler was our horticultural expert and I don't think anyone's been into it since his death. Not that there's much gardening to be done at this time of year. But Jason was really keen; probably it was his way of compensating for not being able to play football or cricket because of his leg. He'd had osteomyelitis as a small child which had left the bone in a weakened state. He became quite proprietorial about the garden and resented other boys going in. If the school manages to survive, I think it should be turned into a memorial to him."

"I met his brother in the Pheasant when I was down last week."

"Toby's a nice youth. He was terribly upset by Jason's death. He's a student at the Knowlton College of Business Studies not far from here. The parents, who live abroad, wanted the two boys to be near each other."

They reached the main front-door and followed Sally Brigstock inside. There was a small closet on the left and she kicked off her shoes and hung up her coat. After putting on a pair of indoor shoes, she led the way down a long passage.

"We can talk in here," she said, opening a door halfway along. "It's the official drawing-room, designed to make a good impression on visiting parents." She flopped into an armchair. "Sit where you like and tell me what you want to talk about."

Challenged in this way, Rosa found herself uncertain where to begin. She hadn't prepared herself for a face-to-face confrontation with the headmaster's wife.

Picking her words with care, she said, "As you're aware, I recently defended Philip Atherly on a drugs charge—"

"He told me how good you were," Sally Brigstock broke in.

"I didn't have a great deal to do." She paused. "Am I right in thinking that you were in touch with him right up to the time of his death?"

"It was I who discovered the body," she replied with a small shiver.

"Yes, I know . . ."

"We first met when he was a master here and I had just become the headmaster's wife." She pulled a face as though it weren't a happy recollection. "We had an affair which we both enjoyed and then Philip left at the end of that term."

"Was that because of the affair?"

"Certainly. My husband got wind of it and told Philip to leave. Actually, there was another reason as well."

"Did that concern Colonel Fox's daughter?"

"So you've heard about that, too! Philip was a good lover, but he never pretended to be a hundred per cent faithful. And I certainly never tried to shackle him."

"And you continued to see each other after he left the school?"

"Yes, when it suited us."

"I take it your husband was unaware of further meetings?"

"Yes."

"Until recently perhaps?"

"Just so. If we'd met only in London, he wouldn't have found out, but we used to meet down here as well."

"In the old summer-house?"

"Among other places. Philip used to get a kick out of sex in unlikely places."

"Were you very much in love with him?"

"Is that a trap question? Are you hoping I'll admit to having a motive for murdering Philip? Because if so, the police have already tried and failed." Her tone was suddenly defiant and her face had assumed a pinched look. Then she gave an impatient shrug. "As a matter of fact, I'm not a jealous person by nature. I never tried to exert any emotional hold over Philip." She glanced at her watch and said brusquely, "The match will be over shortly."

"We must be going, anyway," Rosa said.

"You might find it more difficult explaining your presence to my husband than you have to me, though you've never actually told me the precise reason for your visit."

"Let's say I'm a seeker after truth," Rosa replied.

"What I don't understand," Peter said as they drove back along the mist-shrouded avenue of trees, "is why Atherly used to come and visit her here. I'd have thought London was a much less risky place to meet."

"It may have had something to do with the kinky sex angle."

"I'd hardly call copulating in a draughty summer-house in November kinky."

"The summer-house, as I understand it, was only a meeting place. They'd have gone somewhere else for their sex."

"Like the end of Brighton pier, I suppose." They reached the end of the school drive and he said, "I suggest we go and look up Toby Cutler."

"What's our excuse for doing that?"

"The search for truth, you called it just now."

"But we must have some reason for

barging in on him and asking a lot of questions."

"All right. You're a lawyer with a professional interest in events at Easter House School and I'm your assistant covering the international angles."

Rosa laughed. "But I've no idea where the college is."

"I have. I enquired at the pub where we had lunch. I know exactly how to get there."

Rosa threw him a respectful look before leaning back and staring at some horses grazing in a field, apparently unconcerned by the absence of sun and visibility.

About half an hour later, a large printed board, rising above a hedge, proclaimed "The Knowlton College of Business Studies".

They turned in between two stone pillars and drove up to a rambling Tudor house which was flanked by a number of prefabricated huts. Ignoring the sign that pointed to the car park, Peter stopped the car outside the porticoed entrance. The whole place had a deserted air.

"They probably all go away at weekends," Rosa said, as she prepared to get out.

She walked up to the front door and pressed a bell labelled "Visitors". She was about to do so a second time when the door opened and a young man in a string vest and distressed jeans appeared. It seemed inappropriate garb for a cold day, but he was obviously oblivious of the weather.

"Have you been ringing long?" he enquired.

"No."

"That's as well, because nobody'll answer the door anyway. All the students are away for the day and the domestic staff is putting its feet up. Is there anything I can do to help?".

"I was hoping to find Toby Cutler."

He looked at her sharply. "You're nothing to do with the police, are you?"

"No. Why do you ask?"

"Toby's got a bit jumpy about the police paying him surprise visits. Are you a friend, then?"

"Not exactly."

The young man assumed a puzzled

expression. "You're making it sound rather mysterious."

"If Toby Cutler's not available, I won't waste your time further," Rosa said with a touch of exasperation.

"I never said that. It's just that Toby's friends try and protect him from being harassed."

"Very estimable, I'm sure."

"There's no need to be sarcastic."

"I'm sorry, but I don't seem to be making much headway. Is Toby Cutler here or not? If he is, will you tell him that I'd like to see him?"

"The first answer is 'yes'; the second is if you tell me your name I'll go and find out if he wants to see *you*."

"My name's Rosa Epton and I'm a solicitor from London." She was about to add, "And I'm not here to harass anyone," but decided her visit would probably be interpreted that way by the guardian figure who stood in front of her.

"Is that your chauffeur?" he asked, nodding towards Peter who was still sitting in the car.

"Yes, but he doesn't wear his uniform on Saturdays."

The young man gave her a suspicious look. "You're being sarcastic again," he said after a pause.

"And you, if I may say so, are not being particularly helpful."

"I'm not sure I'll be doing the right thing, but I'll go and tell Toby you're here. Do you want me to say what your business is?"

"I don't see how you can, if you don't know."

He flushed and Rosa half expected him to disappear inside and slam the door. Moreover, she didn't particularly mind if he did.

After he had retreated inside the house, Rosa went across to report to a curious Peter.

"I'd better be on hand for the next round," he remarked, opening the car door and getting out.

"There mayn't be another. Toby Cutler may opt to stay inside his fortress."

Peter shook his head. "He'll appear all right."

As he spoke, the front door opened and Toby Cutler came out.

"Hello," he said in a muted tone.

Rosa gave him a friendly smile. "We met in the bar of the Pheasant."

"I remember."

"Would it be possible to talk somewhere? We could either sit in the car or go for a drive, whatever you prefer."

"There's a visitors' room here which is unoccupied."

"Fine. By the way, this is a friend, Peter Chen. He's also a solicitor."

As Toby led the way inside, his guardian angel turned to follow them.

"It's OK, Ziggy, I'll be all right," Toby said.

It was with obvious reluctance that Ziggy retired from the scene.

"He's a very zealous friend," Rosa remarked, as they entered a room that had all the charm of a second-hand furniture store.

"He and I are about the only two students here this afternoon. Most are off to London or to Brighton. It's a good opportunity to get some work done."

"I'm afraid we've interrupted."

"I was only dictating some notes on to a tape," he said with a weary sigh. "My concentration's all to pot these days and it'll be a miracle if I pass the end of term exams. Fortunately, they're not vital to one's diploma and Mr. Knowlton—he's the principal—knows about all the distractions I've had. In fact, after my brother's death, he suggested I take the rest of the term off. But I felt that would be running away." He pulled a wry face. "And one's always told that running away solves nothing."

"It solves a lot if you're being chased by someone with a sharp knife and you happen to be the more fleet of foot," Peter remarked.

"Is that some sort of a Chinese proverb?" Toby asked with a slight frown.

"No, just ordinary common sense."

Toby appeared to consider this for a moment, then turned to Rosa and said, "I've been thinking about what you said when we met in the pub last week. About Jason being used by Mrs. Brigstock to convey messages to her lover boy. I now think it's more than feasible. It means that on the evening my brother was killed, she was due to meet Atherly, but found herself unable to do so for some reason and sent

Jason to tell him. The poor kid must have dashed out straight in front of the car."

"In that event, the old summer-house wouldn't have been the rendezvous."

"Why do you say that?"

"Because it lies within school bounds and Jason wouldn't have needed to cross the road to reach it."

"Maybe they met in different places to avoid detection," Toby said after a reflective pause.

"I gather you now accept that Jason probably did know Atherly."

"Yes, but why do you put it like that?"

"Because when we met before, your immediate reaction was to reject the possibility. I was also unaware at that time of the note found in your brother's locker. The note that exhorted him to keep up the good work and was signed P. It was accompanied by £5."

It seemed to Rosa that Toby's facial muscles suddenly stiffened.

"I don't get your drift," he said coldly.

"I gather everything points to the note having been written by Atherly and P, of course, would have stood for Philip."

He turned away with a shrug, as though indifferent to the suggestion. When it became clear that he wasn't going to respond further, Rosa spoke again.

"Had you heard of Philip Atherly before he was killed?"

"Heard of him? . . . Well, yes, because he used to teach at Easter House School."

"But that was before your brother went there."

"Yes, but his memory lingered on," he said, with what appeared to be a quick sigh of relief. "Everybody knew about his affair with the headmaster's wife."

"Did you ever happen to meet him?"

"Not that I know," he said, avoiding Rosa's eye. "One meets dozens of people whose names never stick and Philip is quite a common name."

So he did know him, Rosa reflected. Otherwise, why all the flannelling? And if he knew him, why does he want to hide the fact? She decided that Toby Cutler was not the straightforward young man he might wish to appear.

Toby glanced at a clock above the

fireplace and then somewhat pointedly out of the window.

"We mustn't keep you from your studies," Rosa said, getting up.

"I suppose I ought to get back to my desk," he said, springing to his feet.

"Are there any female students here?" Peter enquired.

"No. Mr. Knowlton would sooner close the place than take girls. He's a bit of a sexist."

"Are you allowed to entertain girls on the premises?"

"They're not officially banned, but who'd want to bring a girl-friend here anyway? Though as a matter of fact . . ." His voice trailed away. "Oh, nothing!" he said as if placing a sudden clamp on his tongue.

Five minutes later, Rosa and Peter were back in the car.

"He certainly knows more than he's prepared to say," Peter remarked as they drove off.

"The trouble is he's not the only one," Rosa retorted. "Nevertheless, it's been quite an instructive day."

"I wonder if the police have searched

Cutler's room?" Peter said in a musing sort of tone.

"Looking for what?"

"Evidence of murder. What else?"

18

THE weather the next day was in total contrast to that encountered in Sussex the previous one. The sky was a clear blue and the sun shone brightly, so that it was almost as good as a good summer's day and much better than many.

Peter picked Rosa up around twelve thirty and after a leisurely lunch at a nearby Italian restaurant, they went for a walk in Kensington Gardens which seemed to have become a mecca for half the capital's population. It was getting dark before they returned to Rosa's flat and idled away the evening in pursuit of diverse pleasures.

It was Monday afternoon, just after Rosa had got back to the office from court, that Peter phoned.

"I've found out Joanna Fox's address," he announced. "It's 4A Williford Court, Williford Street, SW7. Not far from Harrods. She lives with an aunt, a Miss

Fox. Why not get in touch with her?"

"I shall, but how did you find all this out?"

"It wasn't very difficult," Peter said airily. "I phoned the Foxes' house at Oakway and spoke to the cleaning lady who answered. I said I'd mislaid Joanna's London address and needed to get in touch with her and could she please give it to me. She was a bit hesitant at first, but I soon persuaded her I was honest and above board and she told me what I wanted to know."

"It was fortunate the Colonel didn't answer."

"In that event I'd have rung off and tried again later. Anyway, there's usually more than one way of finding out something," he added complacently.

"Well, thanks, Peter. I'll call her from home this evening."

"You wouldn't like to come to Geneva for a couple of days, would you?" he asked.

"I'd love to, but I can't. I've got too much work. I take it you mean this week?"

"Tonight, actually. One of my Middle

Eastern clients has summoned me to an urgent meeting."

"Has a nought dropped off his bank balance?"

"Near enough. One of his aides has mislaid three million dollars."

"Mislaid?" Rosa echoed.

"You know how easy it is to do. Anyway, I'll be back on Wednesday, so keep that evening free for dinner."

"I might even cook you scrambled eggs."

"I can't wait. And while I'm away, remember that I love you."

"I'll try, though for two whole days . . ."

At eight thirty that evening she put through a call to the flat in Williford Court. The phone was answered promptly by a voice that sounded young and more likely to belong to the niece than to the aunt.

"May I speak to Miss Joanna Fox, please?" Rosa said.

There was a moment's pause before the voice said, "Who is it?"

"Rosa Epton. I'm a solicitor and I've become professionally involved in a murder case at Oakway. I'd very much like to have a word with Miss Fox."

There was another pause and Rosa could almost see the owner of the voice trying to decide what to do.

"I am Joanna Fox," she said at last. "What is it you want to talk about?"

"It would be easiest if we could meet, Miss Fox," Rosa said in what she hoped was a persuasive tone. "Would that be possible?"

"Oh, I'm really not sure . . . you see, I'm at work all day and I don't go out much in the evenings."

"Do you have a lunch break?"

"Not a regular one. It depends on what my employer requires me to do each day. Sometimes I just have a sandwich at his house, other times I don't bother at all."

"Could we meet one evening after you finish work?"

"Well—"

"It could be anywhere convenient to you," Rosa said quickly.

"When do you have in mind?"

"Tomorrow."

"Oh, I don't think I could tomorrow—"

"What about Wednesday, then?"

"Actually my aunt is out to bridge that afternoon and won't be home till seven thirty so you could come here. But it wouldn't have to take long and I'm afraid you'd have to go before my aunt returned."

"Of course."

"Could you come just before six?"

"Yes, that would suit me fine. Shall I give you my number in case you wish to alter the arrangement? I'll give you both my office and my home number."

There had been several moments during their conversation when Rosa had feared the girl was about to back off. It was, of course, possible that she might still do so.

Williford Street led into one of Knightsbridge's squares where only the rich could afford to live. It was quite short and was dominated by Williford Court, a modern block of flats which stood at one end. The lobby was palatial and thickly carpeted and was under the watchful eye of a stern-looking porter in a dark blue uniform.

"Miss Fox in flat 4A is expecting me," Rosa said, as she reached the desk at which he sat like a dispenser of justice.

"Fourth floor," he said, giving Rosa a

look that clearly imprinted her on his mind for all time. "The lift is over there."

The door of 4A turned out to be directly opposite her when Rosa got out of the lift. She pressed the bell and waited. It was exactly six o'clock.

She had not heard a sound, but suddenly a voice on the other side of the door said, "Who is it?"

"Rosa Epton."

There was the rattle of a chain, then a key was turned and the door opened.

For a moment the two women stared at one another.

"I forgot to tell you that the entry phone is out of order. I'm glad you got in all right. Sometimes undesirables get into the building, so I always ask who it is before opening the door." She stood aside to let Rosa enter, after which she relocked the door and put the chain on.

"I wouldn't have thought any undesirables could get past your porter," Rosa said with a friendly smile.

"They get in through the basement garage. It's only happened once on this floor. My aunt came across a drunk in the corridor. She hit him with her handbag and knocked him over, before sending for help."

Rosa wondered which of them had been in greater need of help.

Joanna led the way into a comfortably furnished drawing-room.

"I hope you won't mind if I don't offer you a drink, but I'd sooner my aunt didn't discover I'd had a visitor. She'd want to know who and why, and I'm not terribly good at lying."

"I quite understand. It's good of you to agree to see me at all." She paused. "Not long before his death I defended Philip Atherly on a minor drugs charge. Then after he'd been murdered, a friend of his named Charlotte Bailey came to see me and said he'd specifically asked that I should investigate his death if and when it took place. It seemed he knew he was in some sort of danger."

While she spoke, Rosa watched Joanna's expression which remained one of polite interest. She had a pair of large grey eyes which never left Rosa's face and she sat perfectly still. Rosa reflected that if she cared to take a bit of trouble with her hair and face generally, she could be a very attractive girl. As it was, nothing could diminish the beauty of her eyes.

Rosa now went on, "I've been down to Oakway a couple of times to nose around a bit and I've met some of the people who live in the area. Mrs. Brigstock and Toby Cutler and the couple who run the Pheasant. Your father was in there on one occasion, but I didn't speak to him." She gave Joanna a tentative glance. "I'm nothing to do with the police and, as far as I know, they're unaware of my interest. It would certainly save me a lot of trouble if they arrested someone in connection with Atherly's murder."

"Even if it was the wrong person?"

"Ah! Do you think there's any danger of that?"

"It can happen, I gather. The police are not infallible."

"And you believe it's a possibility where Atherly's death is concerned?"

"How should I know? I don't live there any more and when I go down at weekends it's not a topic of conversation."

"I gather your mother's an invalid?"

"Yes. She's really the only reason I go down."

"I realise I may be treading on delicate ground," Rosa said, "but I've heard about the ordeal you suffered at Philip Atherly's hands some years ago . . ."

"It wasn't only at *his* hands." Rosa gave her a puzzled look and Joanna went on, "I know he was the original cause of everything, but the worst part came later. The abortion which my father insisted on, followed by all the sessions with therapists and psychiatrists."

"It must have been ghastly," Rosa said earnestly. "May I ask you this, have you ever been in touch with Philip Atherly since it happened?"

She shook her head slowly. "No. He passed completely out of my life. It was like having a limb amputated, but you don't put the severed bit in a drawer as a keepsake, do you?"

"Might your father have believed you'd been seeing him again recently?"

It was Joanna's turn to look puzzled.

"I'm sure not. Why?"

"When I was down at Oakway last Saturday, I heard a rumour to that effect."

"Where?"

"In the Pheasant."

"Was it the only rumour going around?"

Rosa shook her head. "The whole village is rife with them."

"Were there any others concerning my father?"

There was something in Joanna's manner that put Rosa on guard. She felt it was important to make the right answer, as this would dictate the course of their further conversation.

"No, I didn't hear anything else affecting your father," she said in a tone that clearly invited the girl to go on.

"Oh."

"I know your father swore vengeance of a sort against Atherly after what happened, but surely that's now in the past. As far as I'm aware, the police don't regard him as a serious suspect."

"Well, that's their business," she said with surprising sharpness. "In any event, my father's well able to look after himself. It's a pity I didn't inherit some of his toughness." She gave Rosa a wistful smile.

"Slap me down if I'm being too pushy," Rosa said, "but do *you* believe your father was in some way involved in Philip Atherly's death?"

"'In some way involved'," Joanna repeated in a thoughtful voice. She appeared to be racked with indecision whether to say what was obviously on her mind. When she did speak it was to tell Rosa of the discovery she had made concerning one of her father's guns.

"I've been wanting to tell somebody and now I have," she said when she finished. "I couldn't bring myself to go to the police and I didn't know whom I could talk to about it. It's really the only reason I agreed to see you; not that I'd finally made up my mind to tell you until a moment ago." She gave a small shrug. "I suppose I'd subconsciously decided to tell you if you seemed a sympathetic sort of person. You'd sounded one on the phone, but that might have been a lawyer's artifice."

Rosa smiled wryly. "I promise I won't use the information without first speaking to you."

"You can do whatever you like with it. There'd be no point in telling you and then saying, 'But don't pass it on to anyone else.'"

Fifteen minutes later, Rosa took her leave, after promising to keep in touch.

It wasn't very long after she left that the telephone rang in the flat.

"Is that you, Joanna?" her father asked. "I've just learnt that that stupid woman who comes to clean on Mondays gave some anonymous caller your address. Silly creature! I've torn her off a strip. Meanwhile, you'd better be on your guard. It could be some damned newspaper trying to stir up trouble. I take it nobody's been pestering you the last day or so?"

"No, definitely not," Joanna replied with a touch of complacence.

"That's all right then," her father said and rang off.

She had vaguely wondered how Rosa had found out where she lived. Now she knew.

Meanwhile, Rosa was on her way home in a taxi. Two things had clearly emerged in the course of her visit. The first was that Joanna had no great love of her father; the second that she even believed he might have committed murder.

19

COLONEL FOX was troubled. He was quite sure of one thing: namely, that whoever had sought Joanna's address in London couldn't be up to any good.

He wished he was able to read his daughter's mind, but found her a strange, secretive girl. He was unable to forget that she had actually asked him if he had killed Atherly; and she hadn't been joking either.

These thoughts passed through his mind after he had spoken to her that Wednesday evening. Perhaps he would call his sister and tell her what had happened. He and Eileen were two of a kind and got on, provided they weren't obliged to spend too long in one another's company. Eileen would know how to see off any interfering journalist who tried to make mischief. As far as he was concerned all journalists made mischief, it was part of their trade.

Meanwhile, however, he had to decide what action, if any, he should now take.

He had never been a person to sit back and wait on events. His aggressive nature, coupled with his military training, made it natural for him to react positively. He had been taught as a young subaltern that "to do nothing was to do something wrong". There had also been a tag about folded hands and fatalism spelling disaster.

He got up from his chair and walked across the hall to the dining-room where an array of decanters stood on the mahogany sideboard. After pouring himself a stiff whisky, he returned to his study and sat down again. His wife was having her supper upstairs so he knew that he wouldn't be disturbed.

Halfway through his drink his mind was made up. He lifted the telephone receiver from its cradle and punched out a number.

"This is Colonel Fox," he said when a voice answered. "I'd like to speak to Detective Chief Inspector Yule."

Yule, who, as usual, had been in no hurry to go home, was still in his office. He glanced at his watch and wondered why the Colonel should be calling him at this hour.

"Good evening, Colonel Fox," he said when the connection was made.

"Is that you, Yule?"

"Chief Inspector Yule here."

"I'd like to have a word with you. Preferably not here and preferably not the police station. Where can we meet?"

"We could talk in one of our cars . . ."

"Good idea. What about the car park behind the church? It'll be deserted at this hour. See you there in about twenty minutes."

Yule put down the receiver and slowly got up. He was intrigued. It was typical of Colonel Fox not to consult his convenience, but to take it for granted he could immediately abandon what he was doing.

Putting a fresh tape into his pocket recorder, he made his way downstairs and out of the station. He sighed thankfully that DI Hart had gone off duty. Whatever it was, he was sure he could handle it more easily on his own.

Colonel Fox was the first to arrive at the rendezvous and parked over in a far corner well away from the entrance. As he had surmised, the car park was empty. In the summer months it was liable to be populated with courting couples who had nowhere else to go. But November wasn't the month for alfresco courting. He switched off his car lights and waited. It was about fifteen minutes later that another car entered the park and came straight over to where he was.

"Good evening, Colonel," Yule said, as he opened the passenger door and got in. "Hope I haven't kept you waiting." He was aware that in fact he had. Moreover it had been deliberate.

"You're probably wondering what this is all about," Colonel Fox said gruffly. "It's something that's been on my mind for some while and which I now feel it my duty to tell you." He paused as he stared straight ahead into the darkness. "It concerns Mrs. Brigstock."

"Yes?"

"I don't wish to make things more difficult for her, but one has a duty to assist the police. I'm aware that you've recently interviewed her again and I therefore assume she's still on your list of suspects, though that's none of my business. The point is that I feel I can no longer keep silent about something that could have a bearing on Atherly's death. It's my duty to speak out."

That's the third time he's referred to his duty, Yule reflected, making sure that his tape recorder was switched on.

"It seems," the Colonel now went on in a tone designed to distance him from recent events, "that Mrs. Brigstock and Atherly had been conducting a clandestine affair for some time. Or perhaps I should say, had resumed an affair begun when he was teaching at the school. It further seems that Atherly was beginning to tire of the relationship, but that Mrs. Brigstock was not—"

"May I ask how you know this?" Yule broke in.

"Mrs. Brigstock herself told me. She said she wanted to make some dramatic gesture so that he would realise how much she loved him and had decided to threaten suicide unless he promised to continue their association. To this end, she asked if she could borrow one of my guns. I, of course, told her it was a thoroughly stupid idea and I tried to talk some sense into her. But the more I tried, the more determined she became. I then pointed out that if she wanted to indulge in dramatic gestures, her husband owned a shotgun. She said she didn't want to use his as he might find out and their marriage was in enough trouble without that. To cut the story short, I eventually agreed to lend her a single-barrel shotgun I seldom use."

"Where did you give it her?"

"She came to my home one evening and collected it."

"And did you give her ammunition as well?"

"Certainly not. I wouldn't be so irresponsible." The Colonel's voice was coldly indignant.

"But I suppose you knew that Mr. Brigstock kept a supply of cartridges for his gun?"

"If that's a question, the answer is that I have no idea. I imagine it's something you'll have found out in the course of your enquiries."

When asked awkward questions, counter-attack, Yule reflected. Colonel Fox wouldn't be an easy man to corner.

"And what arrangement was made for the return of the gun?" he enquired.

"She was to bring it back as soon as . . . as soon as it had served its purpose. By which I mean, she had used it in her little game of emotional blackmail."

"And did she bring it back?"

"No. She phoned me the day after the murder, by which time I'd already heard what had happened, and told me what I gather has been her story ever since. Namely, that she arrived at the rendezvous to find Atherly lying dead. She said she'd hidden my gun in a pile of logs on her way back to the school and I retrieved it from there after dark that evening."

"And presumably you examined it when you got home?" Yule said, turning his head and fixing the Colonel with a hard stare in the darkness of the car.

"I gave it a good clean. It's not good for a gun to be left lying out in the damp all night."

"But had it been fired?" Yule asked with a touch of impatience.

Colonel Fox reached for his cigarettes and lit one with slow deliberate movements while Yule waited for an answer.

Eventually the Colonel took a deep

breath and said, "To be absolutely truthful, I can't tell you."

"But you must know," Yule expostulated.

"I didn't want to know," he said flatly. "As I've said, it had been lying out under a pile of damp wood all night and I gave it a thorough clean."

Yule stared at him with a mixture of disbelief, doubt and anger.

"Are you trying to cover up for Mrs. Brigstock?"

"I'm not trying either to incriminate her or cover up for her, as you put it. I'm telling you the facts as I know them, out of a sense of duty."

"Would you repeat what you've just told me in a court of law?"

"Certainly. I wouldn't have said what I have unless I were prepared to stand by it."

"Did you not ask Mrs. Brigstock if she had fired the gun?"

"No."

"Wouldn't it have been the natural thing to ask in the circumstances?"

"If she had fired it, I preferred not to know. Whether she'd have told me the truth or have lied, it was better not to ask the question at all."

"Nevertheless, you've decided at this late hour to tell the police?"

"I've explained why. If somebody had already been charged with the murder, I'd have kept my mouth shut. But when I learnt that you'd been interviewing Mrs. Brigstock about an admission she had made to the matron, I decided the time had come for me to speak out."

Yule was thoughtful. If Colonel Fox ever got into the witness-box, the defence would have a field day cross-examining him. Even so, Yule was satisfied that the basic elements of his story were true, which meant that what he had said brought Sally Brigstock's arrest that much closer.

Indeed, when all the bits and pieces that told against her were added together, Yule felt there was enough to justify a charge.

There had always been evidence of motive and opportunity. Now there was considerably more than that.

20

IT was the next afternoon that Rosa learnt of Sally Brigstock's arrest.

As often before, the news reached her via Ben who had slipped out of the office to get the early racing results and returned with a paper containing the news. It was a short item which merely stated that Mrs. Sally Brigstock of Easter House School, Oakway in Sussex, had been charged with the murder of Philip Atherly who had died of gunshot wounds on 20th October. The report added that she would be appearing in court the following day, Friday.

"Like me to come with you, Miss E?" Ben enquired in a hopeful voice. "It's quite a while since I had a day out."

"Come where with me?" Rosa asked, knowing full well what he meant.

"To court tomorrow. You'll be going, won't you?"

"I'll have to think about it. Depends

whether I can put off the case I have at South Western Magistrates' Court."

"Mr. Snaith could probably do it for you," Ben said helpfully. "He's not in court tomorrow."

Rosa laughed. "If I do go, Ben, I shall hardly need your valuable assistance. I shall only be there to listen."

"Pity. If you change your mind . . ."

"I'll let you know."

With a cheerful grin, Ben turned and left her office. A few minutes later, Rosa went along to her partner's room.

"Ben tells me you're not in court tomorrow," she said.

"Ben's right. But I'm about to be propositioned, yes?"

Rosa told him what had happened, adding, "I'd like to be there when she appears."

Robin nodded. "Presumably the police have uncovered further evidence."

"Presumably. Though I still wonder if they've charged the right person."

"From all you've told me about the case, there've always been a number of suspects. The inference is that Mrs. Brig-

246

stock must have edged out of the pack and become the favourite."

"I'm hoping that, although her court appearance tomorrow won't be much more than a formality, I'll be able to glean some information."

"I'd think that's a reasonable prospect. If there's an application for bail, there's sure to be some argy-bargy." After a pause Robin went on, "Not long ago, bail was unheard of in murder cases. Now it's almost commonplace. Mrs. Brigstock should stand quite a good chance of getting out."

"I agree, though I suppose the prosecution is bound to oppose it. But they can hardly suggest she's likely to repeat the offence and, as far as I know, she's never made any attempt to flee while enquiries have been going on."

A train to the nearest mainline station followed by a six-mile taxi ride brought Rosa to Market Welling, the small country town where the justices for the area (which included Oakway) had their court-house.

The first person to greet her as she got

out of the taxi was Jim Thesiger, landlord of the Pheasant.

"Hello," he said affably as Rosa approached. "I had a feeling I might see you here today." With a distinct note of triumph, he went on, "Well, I was right, wasn't I?"

"About what?"

"About it being one of the Brigstocks who'd done it. It's taken the police long enough to decide which. Let's hope they've got the right one."

Rosa made a non-committal noise. "I'd better go and make myself known inside," she murmured, pushing past Jim Thesiger and the throng of interested spectators who were blocking the entrance.

The court-room itself was relatively empty, the public having not yet been admitted. She approached a fraught-looking female who was sorting through papers at the clerk's desk.

"I'm Rosa Epton," she said. "I have a watching brief on behalf of the deceased's family."

Though this wasn't strictly true, she felt it wasn't palpably untrue.

The woman gave her a worried look.

"Oh, we weren't expecting that. I'd better let Mr. Nickson know. He's the clerk, I'm only an assistant." And she scuttled away before Rosa could say anything further.

Noticing a young man sitting at the lawyers' table, Rosa went to join him.

"Are you in the Brigstock case?" he asked with a frown as he glanced up from a volume of law reports open in front of him.

"I'm here on behalf of the deceased's family."

"A bit unusual, isn't it? I mean, at this stage of proceedings."

"Possibly, but I assure you I have no sinister motive. Are you defending?"

"Yes. I'm Barry Hayler. The firm I'm with has its main office in Market Welling."

"Don't tell me if you don't wish to, but are you proposing to apply for bail?"

"Certainly I am. I gather the police will oppose it, but then they always do, don't they?"

"Who's prosecuting?"

"Chap called Bedford-Jones. He can be relied on to make a meal of it."

"In what way?"

"He likes the sound of his own voice. All he has to do today is stand up and apply for a remand. A couple of sentences and he could sit down again. Some hope! You'll think he's opening some government enquiry destined to last into next year."

"Murder cases can affect some advocates that way," Rosa observed.

It was shortly after this that Mr. Bedford-Jones made his appearance, sailing into court as though borne forward by a powerful wind. He was a large man physically, with a florid complexion and a magnificent mane of silvery hair.

"Morning, young Hayler," he greeted his opponent, before casting an interested glance at Rosa.

"She has a watching brief for the deceased's family," Hayler explained.

"Welcome, welcome! The more the merrier!" He held out his hand and warmly shook Rosa's. Turning back to the defence solicitor, he went on, "I take it you're not applying for bail?"

"Then you take it wrong."

"Tch! Isn't that rather a waste of time in a case of this gravity?"

"Not in my view."

Bedford-Jones turned back to Rosa and rolled his eyes heavenwards. "I suppose one must allow youth to have its fling," he murmured indulgently.

Rosa became aware of considerable noise behind her and realised that the public had now been admitted. She looked round to find that every space had been taken and still people were pushing their way in.

A tall, harassed-looking man came and sat down behind Hayler and she recognised him as the headmaster of Easter House School, whom she had last seen charging about a football field in a heavy mist.

Shortly afterwards the clerk entered and took his seat, bestowing nods of recognition on prosecuting and defending lawyers and giving Rosa a quick appraising glance. Almost immediately the usher called for silence and everyone stood as two lay magistrates made their entry. One was a businesslike-looking female, who might have been anything between forty and sixty; the other a male who reminded Rosa of an elderly walrus.

"That's Mrs. Crompton," Hayler

murmured to Rosa. "She's chairman of the bench. Her husband's a chartered accountant."

Rosa nodded her thanks for this information and turned to look at Sally Brigstock who had just been brought into court. Her appearance gave Rosa quite a shock. She had a wild, scared look and it was plain that being charged with murder and spending the night in a police cell had brought home the reality of her situation. She glanced quickly around her, but Rosa noticed that neither she nor her husband made any attempt at communication. He, for his part, sat staring straight ahead of him with a grim expression.

The clerk read out the charge, after which he explained that no plea was required at that stage.

"Your client understands the position, Mr. Hayler?" he enquired at the end of his short exposition.

"I have fully explained it to her, your worships," Hayler said gravely and went on, "There is one further matter I should mention. I apply on behalf of my client for reporting restrictions to be lifted."

There was an immediate buzz of excitement among the assembled newspapermen who weren't expecting to receive this bonus.

The clerk stood up and turned round to hold a quick confabulation with the magistrates whose heads were bent together as in some party game. When he sat down, Mrs. Crompton spoke.

"Very well, Mr. Hayler, we grant your application."

Rosa couldn't help noticing that Mr. Bedford-Jones had also looked smugly pleased in anticipation of being fully reported. Hayler had obviously kept this card to himself before playing it.

In Rosa's experience defending lawyers generally opted to keep reporting restrictions in force, particularly in cases of wide publicity value, in order that an eventual jury shouldn't prejudge any of the issues from what they had read in the papers. The usual reason for applying for the restrictions to be waived was the hope that unknown witnesses might come forward or that publicity would help to flush suspected skeletons out of dark cupboards. She didn't doubt that some of these might be lurking in the present case. She now sat back in her seat with heightened interest.

Mr. Bedford-Jones had meanwhile risen to his feet and, after ensuring he had everyone's attention, began to address the court.

"After a long and painstaking investigation by Detective Chief Inspector Yule and his team of officers, your worships, the defendant, Mrs. Brigstock, was yesterday evening arrested and charged with the murder of Philip Atherly in the grounds of Easter House School at Oakway, not many miles from where we are gathered today. The murder took place on 20th October and Atherly died instantly from the discharge of a shotgun at point-blank range into his face. At the proper time the prosecution will produce evidence that not only did Mrs. Brigstock, who is the wife of the headmaster of Easter House School, have motive and opportunity for the murder, but that she actually borrowed the weapon with which she committed it. Moreover, that she subsequently made certain remarks to the matron of the school which can only be interpreted as admissions of the crime.

"It is the prosecution's contention that this was a most deliberate murder and in those circumstances I now apply for a remand in custody in order that the necessary papers for a committal for trial may be prepared and served."

Though it was true he had said more than was strictly required, he had certainly not gone on for as long as Rosa had been led to expect. He had spoken in the measured tones of one with an eye on the press and he would obviously at a subsequent date say it all over again at much greater length.

Barry Hayler now rose to his feet. "I have no hesitation in applying for bail in this case," he declared, as though half-expecting to be shouted down. "I ask your worships to ignore the tendentious observations of the prosecution. Very little of what Mr. Bedford-Jones has said is accepted by the defence, save that the deceased died of gunshot wounds in the grounds of Easter House School.

"Throughout the investigation, my client has been available to the police for interview. She has made no attempt to run away. They have always known where they could find her. That's the first point. The second is that nobody in their right mind can believe a further murder is likely to be committed if she's granted bail. She completely denies the charge and will present her defence at the proper time. The third point on which I would seek to reassure your worships concerns the question of interference with witnesses.

"There isn't a shred of evidence that the defendant has sought to do so or will do so in future if given her liberty. I'm sure that Detective Chief Inspector Yule will bear out what I say.

"My client can offer substantial sureties and is willing to abide by such bail conditions as the court may see fit to impose."

Barry Hayler sat down and Rosa observed the rivulets of sweat running down the back of his neck. He might have sounded aggressively confident, but nervous tension had turned him into a moist heap.

After a further discussion with the clerk, the chairman announced they would like to hear Chief Inspector Yule.

Yule rose from his seat and made his

way to the witness-box, watched by DI Hart who wore a thunderous expression.

The clerk waited while Yule took the oath. "You heard what Mr. Hayler said to the court?" he asked.

"I did, your worships."

"Do you accept it?"

"No."

"What don't you accept?"

"In my view, the defendant will be under a far stronger temptation to abscond now that she has been charged. Also I believe there's a real danger she might try and interfere with witnesses."

"Rubbish," Hayler observed under his breath.

"A number of witnesses are known to her and live locally . . ."

Barry Hayler now sprang to his feet. "If it will set the Chief Inspector's mind at rest, my client will move out of the area and go and stay with her sister in north London."

"I still object to bail," Yule said quietly.

"Do you have any other ground for opposing it?" the clerk asked.

"The seriousness of the charge."

"I wondered when that was coming," Hayler muttered indignantly.

"Do you wish to question him on it?" the clerk enquired briskly.

"Is it within your knowledge, Chief Inspector, that nowadays bail is frequently granted in murder cases?"

"In certain classes of murder, yes, but not as a general rule."

Hayler sank back into his seat and fanned himself. Meanwhile, the magistrates gathered up their papers and left the bench.

"Do you think they'll give her bail?" an anxious Hayler asked Rosa.

"I've no idea. You know the court better than I do. Quite frankly, I feel a bit sorry for magistrates these days. The Home Office urges a more liberal approach to bail to ease pressure on the prison service, but whatever they do they stand a good chance of being criticised. By the police and the higher judiciary if they grant it and something goes wrong; by the defence fraternity and the civil libertarians if they refuse it when it's a reasonable option. It's a no-win situation." She glanced towards the bench. "Anyway, they're returning to court, so we'll soon know."

As everyone stood up, Rosa turned and looked at Sally Brigstock. Her face was contorted with anxiety as she awaited the decision on her fate.

All eyes were turned on Mrs. Crompton's somewhat skittish hat and the ageing walrus at her side.

"The court has decided," she said in a clear voice, "to grant the defendant bail, subject to two sureties, each in the sum of £5000, who are acceptable to the police. We also make it a condition that the defendant surrenders her passport and reports daily to the police. Finally, we agree with Mr. Hayler's suggestion that the defendant should live away from this area pending future proceedings." She glanced towards the defence solicitor. "Is your client prepared to meet these conditions, Mr. Hayler?"

"She is, your worships," Barry Hayler said, breaking out into a fresh sweat, this time of relief.

Mr. Bedford-Jones had sat throughout with pursed lips and an assumed air of detachment. He had always been adept at dissociating himself from adverse decisions.

"Not my fault, old boy," he was fond of saying to indignant police officers when a decision had gone against the prosecution. "The court'll probably live to regret it."

As Rosa joined the throng pushing its way out of court, she let out a sudden gasp. Just disappearing through the door ahead of her was a face still indelibly imprinted on her mind. Trina Forbes.

By the time Rosa got outside, the girl had vanished. Too late now to wish Ben was with her. For several seconds Rosa stood on the pavement, baffled and frustrated, as she gazed up and down the road with increasing futility.

She was almost ready to believe that she had imagined the whole bizarre incident.

But she knew she hadn't.

21

ROSA travelled back to London in a deeply thoughtful mood. She was still stunned by the unexpected glimpse of Trina Forbes and her mind worked overtime trying to fit her into the puzzle.

She presumed that Trina had been in court the whole time and she cursed her failure to spot her sooner, though it was hardly surprising seeing that the public were herded into the back of the court and the lawyers' table was at the front facing the bench of magistrates.

She wondered whether Trina might have recognised her. Probably not. On the only occasion they had previously seen one another, Trina had been far too absorbed in listening to her tape to register any impression of her fellow passengers. And if she had found Rosa's face familiar, she would have ascribed it to coincidence. She was simply the girl who had sat opposite her in the train from Lewes to London that October afternoon and who now turned out to be a lawyer. So what? She would reasonably infer that Rosa had a local practice.

Rosa was back in her office by early afternoon. The first person she saw as she entered was Ben.

"Hello, Miss E, back already? Hope you didn't regret not taking me," he said cheerfully.

Rosa gave him a jaundiced smile, but refrained from comment.

As soon as she reached her room, she put through a call to the South Midlands Building Society in Northampton and asked to speak to Mrs. Forbes.

"It's Rosa Epton, Mrs. Forbes," she said a trifle breathlessly when the connection was made. "I apologise for calling you at work, but I wondered if you'd had news of Trina?"

"As a matter of fact she phoned two evenings ago, but she didn't say any more than on previous occasions. Just that she was all right and I wasn't to worry."

"Did she say where she was calling from?"

"It was a long-distance call. That's all I know."

"But not an overseas one?"

"It was another bad line and she might have been anywhere. But why are you asking all this?"

"Because I believe I saw her today."

"Saw her? Saw Trina? Where?"

Mrs. Forbes's tone conveyed a mixture of doubt and disbelief.

"In court at a place called Market Welling in Sussex."

"It can't have been Trina. What on earth would she have been doing there?" After a pause, she added anxiously, "You don't mean she was in trouble?"

"No, no. She was there as a spectator. At least, that's what I assume. I only caught a glimpse of her as she was leaving court after the case and then I lost sight of her in the crowd."

"What case are you talking about?"

Rosa explained and concluded, "It would seem she knows someone in the area, because it was in a train from there that I first saw her."

"You don't think she's mixed up in the

263

murder?" Mrs. Forbes said in a strained voice.

"There's no evidence of that," Rosa said with greater confidence than she actually felt. The truth was that she now suspected Trina to have been in some way involved in the events at Easter House School. At the moment she could only make guesses, which could prove to be wide of the mark.

"What do you think I should do?" Mrs. Forbes asked.

"I'm afraid there's not much you can do. I hope Trina will call you again soon and then you can tax her about her whereabouts." Rosa paused before continuing. "Quite frankly, it's difficult to know what you should say to her without having some idea what she's up to. It's one of those situations that can only be played by ear."

"Ought I to phone Inspector Gainham?"

"There's no reason why you shouldn't, though I doubt whether the police will be very interested. Officially interested, that is. You'll be giving them information which merely confirms that Trina is not a missing person. Their official interest ceased the first time she phoned you and showed that she was alive."

"But there must be somebody who's obliged to help us find our daughter?"

"The Salvation Army do a wonderful job tracing young people who have gone missing, but Trina hardly falls within their scope. My guess is that you'll hear from Trina again in the course of the next week and you can ask her point blank what she's doing in Sussex. That could have a cathartic effect."

"I feel myself torn two ways by what she's done. Of course I still love her, but I'm so angry when I think of all the worry she's brought us. However, as you say, there's probably nothing useful we can do except hang on a bit longer."

After she had rung off, Rosa went out into the passage where part of the firm's reference library was housed on somewhat makeshift shelves. They were mostly little-used volumes, which sat gathering dust. She found the book she wanted and returned to her room, where she laid it on her desk and sat down.

It was a comprehensive, though now

out-of-print, work entitled *A Complete Encyclopaedia of Plants*.

"We'll drive down to Oakway this weekend," Peter Chen said eagerly when he and Rosa met that evening and she had given him a detailed account of her day's activities. "Tomorrow, in fact," he added. "The ice has obviously begun to crack and events could start moving fast." He leaned forward and gave her a quick kiss. "Stop the night at my flat and we'll make an early start."

"We never make early starts when I stay with you."

"It needn't be *that* early," he remarked. "We don't want to disturb our priorities."

Rosa giggled, as she was wont to do at the end of a tiring day and after a couple of drinks. They were sitting in the bar of a small Chelsea restaurant. It was still early evening and they were the only customers, apart from two American tourists who had just left the bar and gone to eat.

"We'll order now," Peter said, "then we'll be out before all the yuppies and their girl-friends invade the place."

"You make us sound like the Ancient Mariner and his mother."

Peter bent forward and kissed her again. Rosa decided that if the Ancient Mariner had ever kissed his mother she'd hardly have experienced the same sensual pleasure.

"The barman's watching us," she said with a slight giggle.

"Then he won't want a tip as well. Anyway, hasn't he ever seen two solicitors kissing before?"

It was towards the end of the meal when they had fallen into a joint mood of reflection that Peter broke the silence.

"Colonel Fox sounds a really nasty piece of work. It's obviously his evidence about lending a gun to Sally Brigstock that led the police to charge her. And he can only have told them in order to save his own skin."

"I reckon she's able to look after herself," Rosa observed. "She's never going to hold up her hand and plead guilty, if the case ever gets that far. If she feels in danger of sinking, she'll make sure others go down with her."

"By this time tomorrow, we should

know just how good your guesswork has been."

Rosa made a face. "Converting guesswork into proof, that's the problem. The murderer's had too much time to cover his tracks. It's over a month since Jason Cutler met his death."

The next day was fine. At least, it wasn't raining. The sky was overcast and there was a cold north-east wind.

Rosa and Peter set off in his BMW within half an hour of their intended departure time. Traffic was light and they were in the neighbourhood of Oakway soon after one o'clock. They had no need to stop for refreshment as Peter had cooked an enormous ham omelette before they left. This, with slices of buttered toast and mugs of coffee, would keep them going till evening.

"We're near Knowlton College, aren't we?" Peter said, after they had been twisting and turning along a series of country roads.

"It should be coming up on the right," Rosa replied. "Last time we came on it from the other direction."

"Do you want to stop there?"

Rosa shook her head. "It's best if we stick to our plan."

About three hundred yards farther on, the entrance to the college came into view as they rounded a bend. Somebody was standing by the gatepost; moreover, he was armed with a shotgun.

"It's Ziggy," Rosa exclaimed. "You remember? Toby Cutler's guardian friend."

As they drew level with him, Peter brought the car to a halt and lowered his window.

"What's going on?" he called out.

Ziggy peered myopically at them from the other side of the road.

"You're the couple who came looking for Toby Cutler, aren't you?" he said suspiciously.

"Correct. But what are you doing armed to the teeth?" Peter enquired with a quizzically raised eyebrow.

"I'm hoping to shoot a few rabbits. Mr. Knowlton lets me do it at weekends when everyone else is away. There are usually some in that field opposite."

"Oh! We thought you were on some sort of guard duty."

Ziggy gave them an unamused look.

"If you're looking for Toby, he's not here," he said, plainly hoping that the news would cause dismay.

"As a matter of fact, we're not," Peter replied equably. "Gone away for the weekend, has he?"

"Sort of." Ziggy's tone was curt.

"Well, good luck with the shooting," Peter said, as he prepared to drive on. Closing the window, he added to Rosa, "I wouldn't think the rabbits have much to worry about."

Twenty minutes later, they reached the rear entrance to Easter House School and turned in.

"Zero hour approaches," Peter remarked quietly.

22

RICHARD BRIGSTOCK'S mind was made up. Events, rather than his own untrammelled decision, had dictated his course of action.

The writing on the wall had become starker with the passing of each day since Jason Cutler's death and Philip Atherly's murder had marked a point of no return. Finally, his wife's arrest had spelt the end.

There was no way that Easter House School could continue to survive. If once he had hoped to ride the storm, that prospect no longer existed.

A number of parents had already written to say that their sons would not be returning after the Christmas holiday and now with his wife charged with murder the trickle of withdrawals was bound to become a flood.

The bricks and mortar of the school, together with the grounds, were heavily mortgaged and there was no longer any goodwill to sell. Goodwill, indeed! The word mocked him.

During the Christmas break, he would put his affairs into as much order as possible and then quietly disappear. At 46 he was still young and active enough to start afresh in a new country. He rather fancied South Africa. Somewhere along the line he would probably change his name. . . .

As he sat in his study, turning these sombre thoughts over in his mind, he railed silently against the one person who, above all others, he held responsible for his downfall. His wife. Marrying Sally had proved to be an irretrievable mistake. It was not so much the age difference as their total incompatibility.

So why had he married her, he wondered? At the time it had seemed a good idea. He was a widower in a job where a wife was considered to be an asset. Indeed, more than one set of potential parents had declined to enter their sons for the school on discovering that the headmaster didn't have a wife. Some had expressed pragmatic views on the subject, others said little, but probably harboured uncharitable suspicions.

He had undoubtedly allowed himself to be flattered by Sally's attentions. She was not only young and pretty, but had seemed to have both his and the school's interests at heart. It had never occurred to him that status was what she was really after. That only became apparent later. By the time he realised that he had been taken for a ride, it was too late. Having married her in order to bolster his own position, divorce was out of the question. She had got what she wanted and appearances required that they stick together.

He recalled with a sharp wince of pain the first time he found out about her and Atherly. She had cried a lot and promised that nothing similar would ever happen again. Atherly's departure from the school was meant to ensure that, but had not done so. When he discovered that she had not only kept in touch with Atherly, but was sleeping with him whenever the opportunity arose, his sense of betrayal had turned into explosive anger. Moreover, the fact that it was Atherly who was his wife's lover sharpened his fury. Atherly of all people, a worthless young man of no morals. He would never have offered him a post at the school had he not at the time been desperate for an additional master. He had believed he would be better than nobody and what a disastrous judgment that had proved to be.

Well, Atherly had got his desserts and his wife was about to receive hers. He felt no pity for her, merely a sense of relief that her physical presence had been removed. He certainly had no intention of staying around until her trial. He knew that the prosecution couldn't call him as a witness and there was nothing he was prepared to say on behalf of the defence.

The only reason he had gone to court the previous day was to avoid comment on his absence. He had no wish to stir up speculation about himself. Let the world think he was sitting tight until it suddenly discovered he had gone . . . vanished without trace.

This was the scenario he etched in his mind that late November afternoon, unaware that even as the thoughts fell into place, moles were busily at work not far away.

23

"WHAT we now need more than anything," Rosa said, "is a slice of luck. I'm certain my deductions are right, but we'll need luck in order to prove them."

They were sitting in the car about a mile down the road from Easter House School.

"Bulls in china shops don't need luck," Peter remarked, "and they get results all right."

"They also get a lot of painful splinters in their hides. So what are we going to do?"

"Go to the police and lay all your cards on the table."

"I can't see Chief Inspector Yule being very welcoming. Not after he's just arrested and charged someone with the murder."

"I agree," Peter said with a heavy sigh. "So why don't we drive into Brighton and enjoy ourselves? We can fill our lungs with sea air and decide on our next move. It's an easy place in which to kill time and we could have an earlyish dinner before driving back to town. What do you think?"

"A walk on the seafront sounds quite appealing," Rosa said.

"We could even stop the night," Peter went on brightly. "It won't be difficult to get into a hotel at this time of year."

"But we haven't brought any overnight things with us."

"We can buy a toothbrush there."

"Only one?"

"Two, if you're fussy."

"The hotel might lift a few eyebrows."

"Once a hotel has seen one's money or a selection of credit cards, their eyebrows stay put."

Twenty minutes later they had entered the town and were driving towards the seafront. Rosa, who had sat silent throughout the short journey, let out a sudden cry.

"Stop!"

They had just pulled away from a set of traffic lights and Peter drew quickly into the side of the road.

"What's up?"

"That poster we just passed at the lights. I want to go and take a closer look at it."

"It was for a pop concert."

"I know. But what date?"

"I didn't see. So what?"

"I'll tell you in a minute," Rosa said, getting out of the car and walking twenty yards back up the road, while Peter kept a watchful eye on her in the rear-view mirror. He saw her study the poster for a few seconds before she turned away and came hurrying back.

"It's The Stance," she said excitedly, "and they're giving a concert tonight. It could be our slice of luck."

"Start at the beginning and explain what you're talking about."

Which was what Rosa then did.

Four hours later, they arrived at the venue for the concert. They had driven there immediately after Rosa's discovery and had bought a couple of tickets. She had supposed it would be a sell-out and that they would stand small chance of getting in. She knew that The Stance was a relatively new group and had a substantial following.

Without tickets their quest would have been that much more difficult. Even with them, it still bristled with uncertainty.

After obtaining their tickets, Peter parked the car and they went for a walk along the seafront. Around six o'clock he announced that his breakfast omelette was now a distant memory and that he needed food before facing an evening of raucous music.

"You may find you enjoy it," Rosa said.

"I only like soft, soothing music and they certainly won't provide that," he remarked firmly.

Accordingly they made their way to one of the town's excellent fish restaurants where they ate smoked salmon and drank white wine. Thus fortified, they repaired to the hall where the concert was due to begin at seven thirty.

As that hour approached, Rosa found herself assailed with doubts about what they were undertaking. What had seemed like a slice of luck now had more the air of erratic speculation.

"I just hope I'm not wasting our time,"

she said in a worried voice as they left the restaurant.

"Most of life is spent wasting time, either voluntarily or involuntarily. So don't worry. We've had a nice breath of sea air and the smoked salmon was excellent. What's it matter if things don't work out as you hope this evening?"

"It matters to me."

"Just relax," he said, taking her hand and giving it a comforting squeeze.

Rosa stared about her keenly as they entered the hall, which was rapidly filling. The noise was already considerable, though destined to become much greater once the concert got under way. They found their seats and stared about them at the rows of animated faces.

"It'll be like looking for a needle in a haystack," Rosa said despairingly.

"What else did you expect? Your slice of luck wasn't likely to extend to our finding ourselves in the same row."

"I know."

As the concert got into its stride, Rosa had the impression of being at some tribal ceremony with the audience becoming more hyped up with each number. The trouble was that the constant rhythmic movement of the audience made it impossible to scan the sea of faces. It was like trying to read a book on a bumpy bus ride.

Eventually an interval came and the audience streamed out in search of food and drink, or just plain fresh air.

Rosa and Peter were edging their way towards one of the side exits when she suddenly gripped his arm.

"There, Peter!" she exclaimed, indicating the door they were heading towards. "They're just going out. It's definitely them."

They had no more chance, however, of catching up with their quarry than of defying gravity.

"We'll hang around here," Peter said when they eventually reached the exit. "The odds are they'll come back by the same door. Did you see which row they were sitting in?"

"No. I only saw them as they were leaving."

"And you've no doubt it's them?"

"None."

Fifteen minutes later the hall began to refill for the second half. Rosa and Peter positioned themselves at the door like tellers, counting the faithful.

"They must have come back a different way," Rosa said dejectedly, as the stream of returning fans became a trickle.

"Don't be too sure," Peter said, as a young couple came hurrying across the road in their direction.

He moved across the doorway to confront them while they attempted to brush past him.

A scowling Toby Cutler halted in his tracks as Rosa moved to Peter's side.

"I wouldn't have thought this was your scene," he said in an unfriendly tone.

"We want to talk to you," Peter said.

"After the concert, if you must."

"No, now."

"Don't be bloody silly! If you don't get out of the way, I'll land you one."

"Now that would be silly," Peter said in a steely voice. He turned to Rosa. "You'd better explain to him."

"We want to talk to you about Philip Atherly's murder—"

"I know no more than I've already told you," he broke in angrily. "Now piss off or I'll get one of the security guards." He took hold of the girl's arm. "Come on, Trina, we don't have to put up with this sort of aggro."

"If you go inside that hall," Rosa said slowly, "I'll make sure the police are waiting for you when you come out."

Toby Cutler glowered. "Why the hell can't you stop poking your nose into other people's business?"

"Because Philip Atherly was my client and you murdered him."

24

SEEING Trina Forbes at court had convinced Rosa that Toby Cutler was her connection with Sussex. She had obviously been present in order to report to him on what took place. It was understandable that he wouldn't have wished to show his own interest in the proceedings.

And then earlier that very day when they had stopped outside the entrance to the college, Ziggy had said in answer to Peter's enquiry whether Toby was away for the weekend, "Sort of." It was a curious reply to a straightforward question and Rosa had immediately inferred that he was somewhere with Trina.

Finally, there had been the poster advertising The Stance's concert that evening and Rosa had recalled how the first time she met Toby at the Pheasant, Gina had remarked that he looked in need of cheering up and she would put on a tape of his favourite group, The Stance.

The one thing, however, that she and

Peter had not got round to thinking about was where they would be able to talk in the seemingly unlikely event of her hunch paying off.

The result was some fierce psychological jockeying for control of the situation as they stood outside the now closed doors of the concert hall.

Being Saturday evening, any public building was out of the question. Privacy was their prime consideration, so where could they go?

Toby and Trina said nothing to help solve the problem, no doubt hoping this might be their let-out. The fact, however, that they made no effort to leave seemed to show that they had accepted the realities of their plight.

Finally, Trina had been forced to agree they could go to the room she had rented in an area of bed-sitterland. It turned out that the landlady was away for the weekend, as were two of her fellow lodgers, though this information was extracted from her only with difficulty.

They drove to the house in Peter's car and trooped upstairs in grim silence to her room. She and Toby immediately sat down on the bed, leaving Rosa and Peter to balance themselves on a precariously tilted chaise-longue.

"OK, go ahead, it's your party," Toby said belligerently, as he glared at Rosa.

Rosa nodded. "All right, I'll tell you exactly what I believe happened. I may be a bit astray on minor detail, but I'm pretty sure I've got the main facts right.

"The story starts with your brother Jason, who tended the boys' garden with such obsessive, and if I may say so unlikely, care, even allowing for the disability that prevented him from taking part in normal school games. I remember thinking what an unusual schoolboy he was when I first heard about his preoccupation with the garden. But it wasn't until much later that I realised the reason for his devotion to growing plants. Or one particular plant. Cannabis.

"Peter and I visited the garden this afternoon. It appears to have been unattended since Jason's death, but there was evidence of somebody having fairly recently uprooted a number of plants. My guess is it was you, Toby. You didn't want a prying eye to recognise the harmless-looking cannabis plant and start putting two and two together.

"The only thing is that you left one plant behind. It was growing slightly apart from where you pulled up the others and we now have it in the boot of the car. I can show it to you, if you don't believe me."

"Go on," Toby said in a stony voice.

"It's my guess that Jason grew the cannabis for you to sell. I don't know how many purchasers you had, but Philip Atherly was clearly one of them. On the evening Jason met his death, I suspect he broke out of his dormitory to meet you and hand over a supply, when he was knocked down and killed right in front of your eyes—"

Toby let out an anguished cry and buried his face in his hands, while his whole body was convulsed with sobs. Trina flung her arms round him and pulled him tightly against her side.

"Am I right in thinking that Atherly was the driver of the car?" Rosa asked quietly.

"He didn't even slow down afterwards," Toby said in a choked voice. "He just

286

drove on regardless. I vowed then that I'd kill him, *whatever the consequences to myself*."

"Would he have known it was Jason?"

"He said not, but I didn't believe him. He'd been fornicating with Mrs. Brigstock and was in a hurry to get away."

Rosa frowned. "Weren't you going to meet him that evening?"

"Later. Back at the college. But, of course, he never turned up."

Rosa let out a soft sigh. The dam of silence had been breached and she knew from her experience that from now on the difficulty would be to stop Toby talking.

"Did he drive all the way back to London with his car in a damaged state?"

"He'd once worked in the motor trade and had contacts galore. He left the car with one of his dodgy friends in South London to be repaired and resprayed and then sold with false registration particulars."

"How long had you known Atherly?"

"Just over two years. I met him at a party in town. Everyone there was smoking pot and when I mentioned I had a brother who had just gone to Easter House

School, he came up with this idea. He said the boys' garden would be perfect cover and that he'd pay well for a regular supply. He said that nobody would ever find out because hardly anyone knew what a cannabis plant looked like."

Rosa was thoughtful for a moment. "I suppose the letter found in Jason's locker, exhorting him to keep up the good work and enclosing £5, referred to his cannabis growing and not to acting as a messenger between Atherly and Mrs. Brigstock?"

"Yes. Philip sent it to him."

"Did you intend to kill Philip from the moment of Jason's death?"

"Yes. What's more I told him I was going to."

"But he obviously didn't really believe you. Not enough, at any rate, to avoid taking risks."

"He couldn't keep away from the school nymphomaniac, even though he used to say that he was fed up with her and wanted to break things off. He'd told me he was coming down to see her the evening I shot him. All I had to do was get there first."

"And the gun?"

"Ziggy's. But he never knew I used it to kill someone. I cleaned it thoroughly before returning it." He gave Rosa a look that managed to convey an element of defiance. "So what are you proposing to do?"

For a while Rosa sat staring across the room, deep in thought. Then without answering the question she turned her gaze on Trina.

"On the same day that I first read about Jason's death, you and I sat opposite one another in a train."

"I thought I recognised you when I saw you in court yesterday."

"Ever since that first encounter, I've been puzzled to know what caused you to react the way you did just before we reached Victoria Station. You suddenly looked horribly scared, which was in marked contrast to your happy expression during the rest of the journey. And you left the train as if in flight."

Trina gave Toby a quick glance as if seeking his guidance what to say.

"No reason not to tell you," Toby said, "seeing that you appear to know everything else. Whenever Trina came down to see me, I used to make a tape to pass the time for her on her journey home. It was no more than a bit of a laugh. Most of it was a funny story about an imaginary family I'd invented. I'd got one ready for that particular visit, but was interrupted before I'd quite finished. Later I recorded some threats against Atherly's life on the same tape. It was a bit of play-acting, except that I still meant to kill him. Unfortunately, it scared Trina out of her wits, because although she knew what had happened, she never really believed I had the intention to murder him. But the tape persuaded her." He paused and went on, "That's why she had to be right away when it happened. I sent her to Egypt to stay with my parents. Except that they were off on a trip and she had the house to herself for most of the time. She came back of her own accord about ten days ago and has been living here."

Turning to Trina, Rosa said, "Do you realise how much anxiety you've caused your mother?"

"I've kept in touch with her. She knows I'm all right." Her tone was defiant.

Before Rosa could make any comment, Toby Cutler repeated his question.

"What are you proposing to do? Hand me over to the police?"

"Somehow the record has to be put straight," Rosa said slowly. "At the moment an innocent person stands charged with the murder you committed. Fortunately she's on bail, which makes the problem less pressing than it might be. Nevertheless, you must send the police a signed confession telling them how you came to kill Atherly. You can refer them to me for confirmation."

"You say *send*," Toby observed with a quizzical expression.

"As far as I'm concerned you can walk into the police station and give yourself up *or* you can send them a written confession. As long as you do one or the other within seven days, the choice is yours."

"And if I post them a confession, what do I do then? Sit back and wait for them to come for me?"

"That's up to you."

"You mean you wouldn't try and prevent me absconding?"

"Precisely."

"Supposing I disappear without making any confession?"

"I'd go to the police myself and really put the boot in. But somehow I don't think you will."

"And what happens to Trina?"

"If she takes my advice, she'll go home and make peace with her family. I'm sure you don't wish to involve her with the police."

"I need time to think," he said with a note of desperation.

"You have seven days," Rosa replied. "But not an hour longer."

25

"WHAT do you think he'll do?" Rosa asked as she and Peter drove back to London.

"I don't suppose even he can answer that yet. Not after the way you played God with him!"

"Did I really do that?" Rosa said in a worried tone.

"It sounded that way to me."

"You obviously think I mishandled the occasion."

"I think you were very fair. As one would expect God to be."

"I wish you wouldn't keep on saying that."

"I'm sorry, but it was the way it struck me."

"After all, we could have turned him over to the police immediately, but he's been given a chance to decide his own fate. I feel genuinely sorry for him. It must have been a terrible experience seeing his brother mown down; moreover, it must lie heavily on his conscience." She paused and, when Peter didn't say anything, went on, "And don't let's forget that he committed a pretty ruthless murder and that an innocent person has been charged. He can scarcely expect to receive a pat on the back. If he does disappear abroad, he'll have his freedom, though it mayn't avail him very much in the circumstances."

"Any notion of freedom is largely illusory," Peter remarked.

"If he, too, reaches that conclusion, he'll probably give himself up to the police. With a skilful defence and a sympathetic court, he might get the charge reduced to manslaughter on the grounds of provocation, though it'd be stretching the law more than a bit. He might even have a run on diminished responsibility." She fell silent for a moment. "Tell me, Peter, that I wasn't unreasonable over the options I offered him," she said with a note of pleading.

"You were very fair to him, my little Rosa," Peter said, reaching across and giving her hand an affectionate squeeze.

"You really mean that?"

"Yes."

Rosa sat back and let out a quiet sigh. Nevertheless, she knew it would take more than that to dislodge the suggestion she had played God.

She half expected Toby Cutler to make contact with her early in the following week, either to ask for more time to reach a decision or to make a counter-proposal.

But the phone remained silent.

She suppressed an urge to call Mrs. Forbes and find out if Trina had returned home or been in touch with her mother. She told herself, however, that it was none of her business. Not at that stage, anyway.

It was on the Wednesday following their visit to Brighton that Ben burst into Rosa's office brandishing an afternoon paper.

"Read that, Miss E," he said, pointing at an item headed "Shooting Tragedy". Beneath it was a short paragraph that ran:

Nineteen-year-old Toby Cutler, a student at the Knowlton College of Business Studies near Oakway in Sussex, was found shot dead in his room this morning. A gun lay at his side and the police say that his wounds appeared to have been self-inflicted. It is understood that Mr. Cutler had been deeply depressed since his younger brother was killed in a road accident at Oakway a few weeks ago.

"Oh, no," Rosa murmured and then burst into tears while an alarmed Ben dashed off for help.

For several days Rosa felt numbed by Toby Cutler's suicide. It was an option she had failed to foresee and she reproached herself.

"It was always a possibility," Peter said when she told him what had happened.

"Why didn't you tell me what you thought?"

He shrugged. "There didn't seem much point. If it happened, it happened. I'd already upset you by suggesting you'd played God and I didn't want to cause you further worry. Anyway, it was probably the best answer to his problems. After all, he was still a premeditated murderer, even if his victim was a nasty bit of work."

On the day following the report of Cutler's death, Rosa received a call from Detective Chief Inspector Yule.

"I'm phoning about the death of a young man named Toby Cutler—"

"I read about it in the paper," Rosa broke in. "Did he leave a note saying why he killed himself?"

"He left a note, but all it said was, 'Apply to Rosa Epton for details of my death'. We only found it yesterday. It was tucked away in a pocket of the jacket he was wearing." He paused. "So what are you able to tell me, Miss Epton?"

There followed a series of meetings at which Rosa, with Peter in faithful support, explained her involvement in the case, culminating with their visit to Brighton.

She never expected the police to fall about with gratitude, and they didn't. Her information was received with a frosty politeness, but at least it had the effect of bringing about Sally Brigstock's release from further court proceedings.

In the aftermath of all that happened, Rosa had almost forgotten about Charlotte Bailey's existence. A phone call a few days later, however, brought her sharply back into focus.

"I've read in the paper about Toby Cutler's suicide and that it was he who murdered Philip. I now understand why Philip didn't want his death taken at face value." She paused. "You've certainly earned the £2000 he left for you. Shall I bring it to your office tomorrow?"

"I don't want it," Rosa said firmly. "In fact, I won't accept it. What, as far as I was concerned, began with two intriguing enigmas which arose on the same day ended in a full-scale Greek tragedy and acceptance of the money would make it seem even worse. You keep it, though I'm afraid it won't buy you another gold bar."

Charlotte let out a hollow laugh. "The gold bar that isn't, you mean. I heard from the bank yesterday. It's a complete fake. Its colour is about the only thing about it that's gold. God knows how they were taken in by it in the first place, though they did say it was a very professional fake."

"Do you have any idea how it came into Philip's possession?"

"I've done a bit of digging around. It seems that he was involved shortly before I met him in a vast drug-smuggling scheme. He played a vital link in what was for him a one-off operation and demanded to be paid in gold for his part." She sighed. "Only Philip could have fallen for a phony gold bar. Why couldn't he have asked for Krugerands?" She paused. "Anyway, I'll probably sleep easier without a gold bar."

It seemed to Rosa that Philip Atherly had been destined to reach a violent end to his life.

So far as events at Oakway were concerned, she felt he had more to answer for than anyone.

She gazed at her laden in-tray and reached for the topmost file. It was time to get back to normal.

It was about a month later that Colonel Fox went into the Pheasant for an early evening drink. He had kept away from the place during the aftermath of events, but decided that enough time had elapsed for the dust to have settled.

"Evening, Colonel," Jim Thesiger greeted him with a conspiratorial gleam in his eye. "Not seen you around recently."

"No."

"Expect you've 'eard the latest?"

"What latest?"

"About the Brigstock woman."

"What about her?" Colonel Fox asked sharply.

"You remember she went to stay with her sister when the court gave her bail? Well, it seems she's run off with her brother-in-law. I ask you! Her brother-in-law! I reckon 'e must be an even bigger mug than all the other men she's had."

Making a strange choking noise into his glass, the Colonel swallowed his drink and stalked quickly out of the bar, observed by a distinctly thoughtful landlord.

"Well, I'll be damned," Jim murmured to himself.

We hope this Large Print edition gives you the pleasure and enjoyment we ourselves experienced in its publication.

There are now more than 2,000 titles available in this ULVERSCROFT Large print Series. Ask to see a Selection at your nearest library.

The Publisher will be delighted to send you, free of charge, upon request a complete and up-to-date list of all titles available.

Ulverscroft Large Print Books Ltd.
The Green, Bradgate Road
Anstey
Leicestershire
LE7 7FU
England

GUIDE
TO THE COLOUR CODING
OF
ULVERSCROFT BOOKS

Many of our readers have written to us expressing their appreciation for the way in which our colour coding has assisted them in selecting the Ulverscroft books of their choice. To remind everyone of our colour coding— this is as follows:

BLACK COVERS
Mysteries

*

BLUE COVERS
Romances

*

RED COVERS
Adventure Suspense and General Fiction

*

ORANGE COVERS
Westerns

*

GREEN COVERS
Non-Fiction

MYSTERY TITLES
in the
Ulverscroft Large Print Series

Henrietta Who?	*Catherine Aird*
Slight Mourning	*Catherine Aird*
The China Governess	*Margery Allingham*
Coroner's Pidgin	*Margery Allingham*
Crime at Black Dudley	*Margery Allingham*
Look to the Lady	*Margery Allingham*
More Work for the Undertaker	
	Margery Allingham
Death in the Channel	*J. R. L. Anderson*
Death in the City	*J. R. L. Anderson*
Death on the Rocks	*J. R. L. Anderson*
A Sprig of Sea Lavender	*J. R. L. Anderson*
Death of a Poison-Tongue	*Josephine Bell*
Murder Adrift	*George Bellairs*
Strangers Among the Dead	*George Bellairs*
The Case of the Abominable Snowman	
	Nicholas Blake
The Widow's Cruise	*Nicholas Blake*
The Brides of Friedberg	*Gwendoline Butler*
Murder By Proxy	*Harry Carmichael*
Post Mortem	*Harry Carmichael*
Suicide Clause	*Harry Carmichael*
After the Funeral	*Agatha Christie*
The Body in the Library	*Agatha Christie*

A Caribbean Mystery	*Agatha Christie*
Curtain	*Agatha Christie*
The Hound of Death	*Agatha Christie*
The Labours of Hercules	*Agatha Christie*
Murder on the Orient Express	*Agatha Christie*
The Mystery of the Blue Train	*Agatha Christie*
Parker Pyne Investigates	*Agatha Christie*
Peril at End House	*Agatha Christie*
Sleeping Murder	*Agatha Christie*
Sparkling Cyanide	*Agatha Christie*
They Came to Baghdad	*Agatha Christie*
Third Girl	*Agatha Christie*
The Thirteen Problems	*Agatha Christie*
The Black Spiders	*John Creasey*
Death in the Trees	*John Creasey*
The Mark of the Crescent	*John Creasey*
Quarrel with Murder	*John Creasey*
Two for Inspector West	*John Creasey*
His Last Bow	*Sir Arthur Conan Doyle*
The Valley of Fear	*Sir Arthur Conan Doyle*
Dead to the World	*Francis Durbridge*
My Wife Melissa	*Francis Durbridge*
Alive and Dead	*Elizabeth Ferrars*
Breath of Suspicion	*Elizabeth Ferrars*
Drowned Rat	*Elizabeth Ferrars*
Foot in the Grave	*Elizabeth Ferrars*

Murders Anonymous	*Elizabeth Ferrars*
Don't Whistle 'Macbeth'	*David Fletcher*
A Calculated Risk	*Rae Foley*
The Slippery Step	*Rae Foley*
This Woman Wanted	*Rae Foley*
Home to Roost	*Andrew Garve*
The Forgotten Story	*Winston Graham*
Take My Life	*Winston Graham*
At High Risk	*Palma Harcourt*
Dance for Diplomats	*Palma Harcourt*
Count-Down	*Hartley Howard*
The Appleby File	*Michael Innes*
A Connoisseur's Case	*Michael Innes*
Deadline for a Dream	*Bill Knox*
Death Department	*Bill Knox*
Hellspout	*Bill Knox*
The Taste of Proof	*Bill Knox*
The Affacombe Affair	*Elizabeth Lemarchand*
Let or Hindrance	*Elizabeth Lemarchand*
Unhappy Returns	*Elizabeth Lemarchand*
Waxwork	*Peter Lovesey*
Gideon's Drive	*J. J. Marric*
Gideon's Force	*J. J. Marric*
Gideon's Press	*J. J. Marric*
City of Gold and Shadows	*Ellis Peters*
Death to the Landlords!	*Ellis Peters*
Find a Crooked Sixpence	*Estelle Thompson*
A Mischief Past	*Estelle Thompson*

Three Women in the House   Estelle Thompson
Bushranger of the Skies   Arthur Upfield
Cake in the Hat Box   Arthur Upfield
Madman's Bend   Arthur Upfield
Tallant for Disaster   Andrew York
Tallant for Trouble   Andrew York
Cast for Death   Margaret Yorke

FICTION TITLES
in the
Ulverscroft Large Print Series

The Onedin Line: The High Seas
Cyril Abraham

The Onedin Line: The Iron Ships
Cyril Abraham

The Onedin Line: The Shipmaster
Cyril Abraham

The Onedin Line: The Trade Winds
Cyril Abraham

The Enemy   *Desmond Bagley*
Flyaway   *Desmond Bagley*
The Master Idol   *Anthony Burton*
The Navigators   *Anthony Burton*
A Place to Stand   *Anthony Burton*
The Doomsday Carrier   *Victor Canning*
The Cinder Path   *Catherine Cookson*
The Girl   *Catherine Cookson*
The Invisible Cord   *Catherine Cookson*
Life and Mary Ann   *Catherine Cookson*
Maggie Rowan   *Catherine Cookson*
Marriage and Mary Ann   *Catherine Cookson*
Mary Ann's Angels   *Catherine Cookson*
All Over the Town   *R. F. Delderfield*
Jamaica Inn   *Daphne du Maurier*
My Cousin Rachel   *Daphne du Maurier*

Enquiry	*Dick Francis*
Flying Finish	*Dick Francis*
Forfeit	*Dick Francis*
High Stakes	*Dick Francis*
In The Frame	*Dick Francis*
Knock Down	*Dick Francis*
Risk	*Dick Francis*
Band of Brothers	*Ernest K. Gann*
Twilight For The Gods	*Ernest K. Gann*
Army of Shadows	*John Harris*
The Claws of Mercy	*John Harris*
Getaway	*John Harris*
Winter Quarry	*Paul Henissart*
East of Desolation	*Jack Higgins*
In the Hour Before Midnight	*Jack Higgins*
Night Judgement at Sinos	*Jack Higgins*
Wrath of the Lion	*Jack Higgins*
Air Bridge	*Hammond Innes*
A Cleft of Stars	*Geoffrey Jenkins*
A Grue of Ice	*Geoffrey Jenkins*
Beloved Exiles	*Agnes Newton Keith*
Passport to Peril	*James Leasor*
Goodbye California	*Alistair MacLean*
South By Java Head	*Alistair MacLean*
All Other Perils	*Robert MacLeod*
Dragonship	*Robert MacLeod*
A Killing in Malta.	*Robert MacLeod*
A Property in Cyprus	*Robert MacLeod*

By Command of the Viceroy   *Duncan MacNeil*

The Deceivers   *John Masters*

Nightrunners of Bengal   *John Masters*

Emily of New Moon   *L. M. Montgomery*

The '44 Vintage   *Anthony Price*

High Water   *Douglas Reeman*

Rendezvous-South Atlantic   *Douglas Reeman*

Summer Lightning   *Judith Richards*

Louise   *Sarah Shears*

Louise's Daughters   *Sarah Shears*

Louise's Inheritance   *Sarah Shears*

Beyond the Black Stump   *Nevil Shute*

The Healer   *Frank G. Slaughter*

Sword and Scalpel   *Frank G. Slaughter*

Tomorrow's Miracle   *Frank G. Slaughter*

The Burden   *Mary Westmacott*

A Daughter's a Daughter   *Mary Westmacott*

Giant's Bread   *Mary Westmacott*

The Rose and the Yew Tree   *Mary Westmacott*

Every Man a King   *Anne Worboys*

The Serpent and the Staff   *Frank Yerby*

WESTERN TITLES
in the
Ulverscroft Large Print Series

Gone To Texas	*Forrest Carter*
Dakota Boomtown	*Frank Castle*
Hard Texas Trail	*Matt Chisholm*
Bigger Than Texas	*William R. Cox*
From Hide and Horn	*J. T. Edson*
Gunsmoke Thunder	*J. T. Edson*
The Peacemakers	*J. T. Edson*
Wagons to Backsight	*J. T. Edson*
Arizona Ames	*Zane Grey*
The Lost Wagon Train	*Zane Grey*
Nevada	*Zane Grey*
Rim of the Desert	*Ernest Haycox*
Borden Chantry	*Louis L'Amour*
Conagher	*Louis L'Amour*
The First Fast Draw *and*	
The Key-Lock Man	*Louis L'Amour*
Kiowa Trail *and* Killoe	*Louis L'Amour*
The Mountain Valley War	*Louis L'Amour*
The Sackett Brand *and*	
The Lonely Men	*Louis L'Amour*
Taggart	*Louis L'Amour*
Tucker	*Louis L'Amour*
Destination Danger	*Wm. Colt MacDonald*

Powder Smoke Feud

William MacLeod Raine

Shane

Jack Schaefer

A Handful of Men

Robert Wilder

NON-FICTION TITLES
in the
Ulverscroft Large Print Series

No Time for Romance	*Lucilla Andrews*
Life's A Jubilee	*Maud Anson*
Beautiful Just! and	
Bruach Blend	*Lillian Beckwith*
An Autobiography Vol.1	
Vol.2	*Agatha Christie*
Just Here, Doctor	*Robert D. Clifford*
High Hopes	*Norman Croucher*
An Open Book	*Monica Dickens*
Going West with Annabelle	*Molly Douglas*
The Drunken Forest	*Gerald Durrell*
The Garden of the Gods	*Gerald Durrell*
Golden Bats and Pink Pigeons	*Gerald Durrell*
If Only They Could Talk	*James Herriot*
It Shouldn't Happen to a Vet	*James Herriot*
Let Sleeping Vets Lie	*James Herriot*
Vet in a Spin	*James Herriot*
Vet in Harness	*James Herriot*
Vets Might Fly	*James Herriot*
Emma and I	*Sheila Hocken*
White Man Returns	*Agnes Newton Keith*
Flying Nurse	*Robin Miller*
The High Girders	*John Prebble*
The Seventh Commandment	*Sarah Shears*
Zoo Vet	*David Taylor*